For Jorge &
Bonnie

[signature]

PETROS SPATHIS

PETROS SPATHIS

BY MANOLIS

libros libertad
2008

Copyright © Manolis 2008. All rights reserved.

No part of this book may reproduced, stored in a retrieval system, or, transmitted by any means without the written permission of the author.

First published by:
Libros Libertad Publishing Ltd.
PO Box 45089
12851 16th Avenue, Surrey, BC, V4A 9LI
Ph. (604) 838-8796
Fax (604) 536-6819
www.libroslibertad.ca

Library and Archives Cataloguing in Publication

Manolis, 1947–
   Petros Spathis / Manolis

ISBN 978-0-9808979-3-7

1. Title.

PS8626.A673P48 2008   C813'.6   C2007-907549-5

Design and layout by Vancouver Desktop Publishing Centre
Printed in Canada by Printorium Bookworks

About the Author

Manolis was born on the island of Crete in 1947 and was educated in Greece (BA in Political Sciences, Panteion Supreme School of Athens). He served in the armed forces for two years, and emigrated to Vancouver in 1973, after which he worked in several different jobs over the years. He attended Simon Fraser University for a year taking English Literature in a non-degree program. He has written three novels, a number of collections of poetry, which are slowly appearing as published works, various articles and short stories in Greek as well as in English.

After working as an iron worker, train laborer, taxi driver, and stock broker, he now lives in White Rock where he spends his time writing, gardening, and traveling.

Towards the end of 2006 he founded Libros Libertad, an unorthodox and independent publishing company in Surrey, British Columbia with the goal of publishing literary books most other companies reject, thus giving voice to people who are not listened to by conventional publishers.

BOOKS

Stratis Roukounas, novel, (in Greek) 1981 Athens Greece, Mavridis Publishing.

The Orphans, poetry, 2005, Authorhouse, Indiana USA

Footprints in Sandstone, poetry, (2006), Authorhouse, Indiana, USA

Path of Thorns, poetry, (2006), Libros Libertad Publishing, Surrey, B.C.

El Greco—Domenikos Theotokopoulos, poetry (2007) Libros Libertad Publishing, Surrey, B.C.

Praise for the Works of the Author

It's hard to write poetry of affirmation in a post-modernist culture where irony is a compulsive tic. But this new collection by Manolis, a series of meditations on the life and work of the great Cretan artist Domenikos Theotokopoulos (El Greco), triumphs in its lyric intensity and open-hearted transcendentalism. This is a celebration of Hellenic culture and an affirmation of human aspiration amid the chaos of history and the muddle of consensus reality. The poet discovers epiphanies of a heightened vision in the iconography of the paintings. The offset four-line stanza form gives space for reflection and shape to his unfolding narrative.

As the poet enters the space where El Greco worked and sits before the canvasses he's overcome by what the philosopher Colin Wilson calls "Faculty X"—an existential grasp of the actuality of the past as a living present, an intuitive *gnosis*. "The movement of the brush /waves through the air of/ sulphur and darkness." Vivid images from nature are linked with the exalted vision of the painter, creating a Blakean sense of the world as suffused with a divine energy. As we contemplate the paintings, reproduced in the book, our own vision is re-energised and refreshed. —*Paul A. Green*

I believe that people like Conrad, Nabokov, Jonas, Manolis, and Bronowski have an advantage in crossing over from another language; they do things with English words which native speakers would never think of. El Greco illustrates my point superbly.
—*John Skapski*

I think Manolis Aligizakis is the best émigré Greek writer in Canada and I welcome his return to publishing. —*J. Michael Yates*

The Orphans does not intend to change the world; it intends to open the people's eyes. —*Now Newspaper*

I'm touched by the poetry of this man . . . —*Winnie McCormick*

The Orphans definitely stirs up conversation and debate. One doesn't necessary agree with all in this book, yet a few things hit the nail on the head.   —*Chuck Grodzicki*

With smooth wholeness of imagery, with lively characters and detailed descriptions Manolis Aligizakis presents his new novel . . . Stratis Roukounas . . .   —*Aristidis Mavridis, editor in chief,*
     Literary Annual Review, *Athens, Greece*

The writer who is as soft as a summer wind's caress uses as subjects nature, the sea's dancing, his parents, his lineage, his Cretan roots and handles language with pride and responsibility. I never imagined that April shallows reach the northern frozen lands where we live, yet I encountered them as I opened the books of my compatriot. Shallows sprang forth from the words and now reach the readers of our newspaper.

 Manolis' images resemble those old muzzleloaders that get transformed into cherubim by a graceful lyre. Men who were nurtured by the manly Cretan dances, who were tested by the sea's salinity, who quenched their thirst with the sweat of hard physical work could only have as a result this poetic limpidity parallel to none, this poetic transparency that touches even the dead.
    Iris Canea, editor, The Vima, *Toronto Canada*

Path of Thorns is a very powerful collection, addressing universal themes—childhood, love, exile, endurance, death—but grounded in Manolis' experience of civil war in Greece, and migration to Canada. He also explores the paradoxes underlying contemporary global suffering, epitomized in the floods of New Orleans. Yet the final sequence is a mythic celebration of our potential for self-transformation and creativity. In his intense lyricism Manolis pays homage to the Hellenic poetic tradition embodied in writers like Kazantzakis and Elytis, while reminding us of a common humanity that transcends cultures. These poems will resonate with many readers, at many levels."   —*Paul Green*

1

There, then, he sat, holding that imbecile candle in the heart of that almighty forlornness. There, then, he sat, the sign and symbol of a man without faith, hopelessly holding up hope in the midst of despair.

— *Melville*

On the celestial blue wad of uncertain inertia, shapes of water are described by continents. The continents possess invisible lines, separating and protecting nations from the unknown. These are called borders and function as seawalls against meaninglessness. In the capital city of one nation whose border is marine, except for its interior portions that are seldom acknowledged—is a building. Inside the building, which seems made entirely of corridors without destinations—yet with no Minoan puzzle, no labyrinth in mind at its construction—is a small cell, number 322. In the room, so without character, there is one small, barred window to describe a man. In the man are a blue Mediterranean of memory and his imaginary port through which he summons his island: sailing, skewering the centuries at the speed of a wild dove, jagged face sunward, savaging back the battle of glaucous breakers, waking behind a spoor of black blood.

The image intensifies in resolution; a sword-blade geography, an oblique holiness fuelled by ferocity.

It is the slopping of the beasts, or as it is known more formally, the distribution of the evening meal to the prisoners; to Petros Spathis' surprise and pleasure, Vikas' son is on duty, standing there in the doorway of his cell with his tray. The son whispers that things outside the prison are going well, very well, and his father, Colonel Vikas, will come and visit as soon as he can contrive an unsuspicious excuse. With that modicum of lift, Petros Spathis begins the adventure of the evening meal with as much appetite as he can muster.

Then he goes to sit on his bed and write in his diary.

The diary has become a total zodiac of his phases and conjunctions of mind since the beginning. Each deep midnight and each high noon of his mood is logged here. A small dynamism within the large arrest, a faint stirring in the service of sustaining sanity, an unfounded and dangerously nude hope that the words will never die in this placenta of paper.

He stands, face to the wall, and speaks; it must be understood, he does not consider himself isolated. As he stares with such sincerity at a single stone in the wall, it is exactly as if he were endorsing with his eyes all he is saying, as if he were attempting to convince someone of something upon which everything depends. His hands do not lie. Of his thoughts, he remains supremely in command. His judgment filters each act.

The jocular silence modulates his consciousness toward a familiar key, a poem somewhere without exordium. The serenity of a word curving across the page, the nascent thought merging with the nascent hand until the circuit shorts and . . .

> *Vikas, Vikas, Vikas, how ever did you manage it? Everything is going superbly, just as your fine lad said. It is almost as if all this never . . .*

A bolt of energy strikes through him. Exercise. But at this intersection of hour and mood? To him, morning and exercise relate. Now and exercise collide. The commitment of discipline must not loosen, derange, or unfasten him.

As if on command, he arises and stands at attention. His body commands his mind to command: a few knee-bends, then jumping jacks, extend the hands almost to the walls. Inhale deep, exhale slow, his breath becomes cuprous, tarnished, an obese air; but he continues, and his lungs butterfly and collapse, perhaps in rehearsal for a ritual in which he may never take part.

There has been no extraordinary exertion, yet the burden of boredom diminishes him to the figure of a junkman's nag tolling uphill before the overload of relic erudition. Half of a man knows it is war; half of a man insists it isn't. In the confusion it's difficult to discern which enters the theater of war with a plowshare.

The blunder into the hunt, to discover oneself, is a quarry that dogs all degrees of the cosmos.

He stops as abruptly as he started and sits on his bed. His minds flies back to the island.

This is the only occasion that he is able to travel during the day. All other times he had traveled, he would leave at night and arrive at dawn. This time he has the opportunity to enjoy the daytime trip, to admire the blue summer sky, the peaceful sea, and the scenery along the islands so beautiful that it has attracted myriads of foreigners from all corners of the world. It is early April. The mid year exams held end of Febuary every year are finished and it takes at least a month to know the results: it is a great opportunity for him to visit his hometown, to enjoy swimming in the crystal clear virgin sea, and to stay with his folks for a while. Besides, his father may need hands this time of the year with the orchards.

He leans against the railing of the ship, gazing far into the horizon. A few seagulls are flying overhead, keeping the ship company on its voyage. They become the vessel's inseparable companions from the beginning of the trip to the end. He wonders how much strength these birds must have to be able to endure such a journey. There are no clouds anywhere, only small puffs of smoke coming out of the ship's smokestack.

From the other end of the deck come loud voices, and a few children are pointing at something with their little hands and laughing. Petros goes over: it is a school of dolphins playfully jumping in the water. He counts them with a glance—there must be over ten. Amazing! He has seen them all the time since he was little, yet he still can't help feeling enchanted.

He sits on a bench thinking of the island he comes from, his home, his place of birth: the island with its rugged mountains, its warm western seas, its ancient solitude. So strange, so tormented, yet so enchanting is this island, so large and narrow, with its steeply cut seashores, its beautiful beaches, the proud insubordinate mountains, the rolling valleys and vineyards.

A familiar old verse comes back to him, and he quietly murmurs,

> *When on this island,*
> *take it stepping stone by stepping stone*
> *and with each footstep bear in mind*
> *the number of battles,*
> *equals the number of stones.*

As the origins of such verses are untraceable in the timeless villages like the one Petros comes from, he cannot date when it entered him to remain imprinted there forever.

On his face is a smile of satisfaction, of pride, of joy, a certain glow that becomes even brighter under the sunrays of midday. He is truly proud of where he comes from, where people are noble and hospitable, where there is something in them so difficult to describe, the Cretan Glance. The epic element has always been strong here, so that these people are very different from the other Greeks of the mainland, and their souls have always been manly and cannot ever be suppressed. Their hospitality and zeal for honor and nobility are boundless. This rock, this island, their home, has taken thousands of years to be created, with blood, and courage.

These people accustomed to climbing their rugged mountains, through difficult ravines and crevices, to sleep with a rock as a pillow, with their weapons by their side, extensions of their bodies, and rebellious always like their insubordinate mountains. They know they must struggle for life and for death. The willingness for sacrifice is ever present in the depths of their existence.

These people have veins swollen with anxious, boiling blood. These people have eyes with a sweetness you cannot express with words.

The island always welcomes the good-intentioned stranger with the same zeal as it fights its enemies. It is its story, its tradition, its song, to be warm and sharp like the blade of a pirate's sword. It is its story, its tradition, its song with a quick eye and winged feet, while its goat shepherds pass the night close to their small flocks, up on the rough hills. It is a story, a tradition, a song of this island, which becomes spirited at the necessary times and fights with claws and teeth in order to reach its zenith.

Petros' thoughts are interrupted by loud voices a few yards away. He turns and sees two officers restraining three young men; a bit farther away, a girl is lying in a sun chair; she looks foreign. The young men are ardently defending themselves pointing at the girl who is wearing nothing more than her bathing suit. A very pretty young woman indeed, arousing the interest of the young men, who most likely call names at her with the result of her calling the officers to complain.

"Idiots!" thinks Petros.

Petros Spathis' handsome features compliment his twenty-seven years. His dark complexion, eyes, hair, and body have this melodious balance like a well-built athlete seen in brochures and ancient books. His girlfriend, Eleni, of the last two and a half years, escorted him to the harbor before he embarked for the trip to Crete, contrary to his uncle's wish of taking him there himself. Petros insisted so his uncle and auntie said their farewells at home. Eleni and Petros met in a nightclub a couple of years ago in the island of Ios where they were both vacationing. Petros loves to play with her pretty blonde hair, and he mostly enjoys letting his eyes dive deep in her blue eyes.

He walks toward the deck bar passing by the pretty sunbathing tourist girl. It is not easy to walk along with all these people sitting or lying around on the deck.

He orders a cold coffee and glances around. Next to him is an old man drinking his lemonade: hard features, wrinkles on his face, white hair, black circles around his eyes.

The old man feels Petros' glance and turns toward him: "And where are you from young man?"

"From around here, Uncle," Petros answers, imitating the old man's accent. It's customary to address an older man as "Uncle" when one doesn't know his name. Whenever coming to the island, Petros likes to talk with an accent close to the locals' in order to conform to their ways as much as possible.

His coffee is served, and he takes a slow sip to see how good the coffee is. The old man observes his ritual manner, satisfied.

"Can I ask you something, Uncle?" Petros feels the need to kill the silence between them.

"Sure. What is it, my son?"

"The island, why is it called Crete?"

The old man raises his eyebrows. Not many people ask this kind of questions.

"We call it Crete because it means wines and meats."

Petros is surprised. He never knew. Does this mean that this island used to be fertile and fruitful, and the people never had to worry about their food?

The old man turns to ask him.

"What do you do in Athens, my son?"

"I attend the university, Uncle. I am graduating this year."

"Oh, you are a sand pebble then."

"A sand pebble?"

"Yes, you know, one of the few who stand up among all others. We expect you to lead this country someday, and toward a better future I hope."

"Oh, yes, I think I understand now. A sand pebble."

Petros stops for a moment and then asks again.

"And why you think we'll lead this country to a better future? Isn't it heading that way now?"

"No, it is not. We want our country head toward the future we always hope for, Son."

"How do we know we go toward that direction, Uncle?"

"I can't describe to you, Son. You will know it when your heart tells you it is the right way, when you do not sell out who you really are, when you do not compromise your integrity."

"And how will you know you are following all these?"

"Trust me, when the time comes, you will know, my son."

The old man then gets up and leaves.

Long after he is gone, Petros still thinks of his words.

When he goes out to the deck again, the outline of the island becomes more visible. People are standing on deck observing the mountain peaks that touch the sky as the sun shines on them from the west.

He does not know how long he has stood there against the railing of the ship, watching the island slowly getting nearer, watching the immensity of its outline. A feeling of wonder comes over him: the size, the beauty, the firmness. This is not the first time he comes home from the capital, but at this hour, his soul can see things much more: he can understand that his heritage, the flame within him, is lit exactly like the young men of this land who have mastered the art of beautifying their days with a flask of red wine, with imagination, with a pure heart.

Yes, he now understands. It is an art originated in the ancient years, from the ancestors who have faded away but left behind them a flooded stream of light, golden light. And within this light, every moment of the eternal memory of this island is resurrected. The light can be one's imagination, a drunken illusion, or pure poetry like the flowers of wild saffron. The people of the land took this poetry to heart, and with it created the destiny of this land. Crete exists as an infinite twilight among three continents. He stares at this island, his face reflecting supreme exultation, and justified selfishness.

The ship is now making a turn to enter the harbor. Petros can see clearly the steep mountains rising straight from the sea. The dock comes into view. Many other small and large boats are scattered here and there.

The crew is now preparing to dock. There are a lot of people and cars on the wharf. He can see some village men with baggy black breeches tucked in high boots and wearing delicately embroidered vests with black scarves bound around their head; their shaggy hair, thick beards, and long moustaches. When the ship finally docks, Petros can hear them speak a kind of a thick dialect and see their eyes sparkle with stubbornness and virtue. These people are fierce, insubordinate, harsh souls. It is really hard to walk in their footprints.

A few villagers eagerly wait for the gangplank to be lowered so they can rush aboard to greet their loved ones. Petros goes down to the locker room to retrieve his small piece of luggage. Then he steps behind the queue and slowly walks off the ship. His village is about twenty kilometers from the harbor and there is no bus service available at this hour. However, he easily finds a couple of people going the same direction, and they share a taxi together.

Everybody is asleep in the village except those in one coffee shop. When the taxi drops him off, Petros passes by it as he walks to his home. It has been a long day.

His folks did not expect him and his mother almost faints from seeing him at the doorstep.

"My son, is it you? Welcome home. Why didn't you let us know you will be home?"

Not knowing which question to answer first, he kisses her and laughs.

"It was a last minute decision, Mother. A day trip this time: it was beautiful."

His father wakes up from all their noise and comes downstairs.

"Well, well, welcome!"

"How are you, Father?"

"Fine, my boy, but what is this? Have you finished your exams?"

"Yes, Father. I finished everything last week, and the results are not expected for at least a month. That is why I decided to come and see you for a while."

"That is great, my son."

"Would you like me to fix something for you to eat? Are you hungry?" his mother asks eagerly.

"Not this time of the night, Mother. I will go to sleep and tomorrow we will talk again, I am very tired now, alright?"

"Yes, Son, I will go and fix your bed."

As soon as morning arrives, Petros opens his eyes. The sky takes the color of day with the morning star still visible through the misty dawn. Slowly the sun rises and eclipses the star. It is a beautiful morning.

His father has already gone to the orchards, and his mother is anxiously waiting for him to get up so she can talk to him, so she can look at him, so she can look at her first and only child who is a man now, a graduate from the university, her pride. All night she wondered about what to prepare for him, what to treat him with. She knows well how difficult it is for him away from his mother's touch while studying in the city, attending classes, writing exams, and all. She has prepared some cheese pies of her own recipe with lots of sugar and cinnamon which she knows he loves. She expects him to rise late since he had traveled all day. She fixes his coffee and walks to his bedroom. To her surprise he is not only awake, but also dressed.

Petros' father, George Spathis, is a fifty-two-year-old man who grew up in the orphanage, placed there by his mother, a young unmarried woman. George grew up in the orphanage until he reached the age of eighteen, when he went back to the village where his mother and natural father lived. He has two step-siblings on his mother's side: a brother, Demetre, who lives in Athens, where Petros stays while at school, and a sister, Katerina, who lives someplace in Germany. He also has a few step-siblings from his natural father's side, but his father has never told Petros how many there are and whether they have any children. Petros' father is a reticent man, and it is rare to be able to start a conversation with him. It is Petros' mother, Despina, who told him the story about his father and how they got married soon after he came back to the village from the orphanage. Despina is a chubby sixty-four-year-old woman, a saint, as her son thinks of her. She has only love in her heart, so much love for everyone but mostly for her only son Petros, who is her pride.

"Oh, Mother," he says affectionately and embraces her. "I will have to leave you soon after breakfast because I need to go up to the monastery. I promise we will have a long talk when I come back."

"Why do you need to go to the monastery, Son?"

"I need to look for something in their library. I will go by the orchards to say good morning to Father first and then carry on from there. I will be back for lunch."

He finishes his coffee, eats one cheese pie, and says goodbye to his mother. He chooses to walk in the fields by the olive grove, surrounded by the harmonious chirps of the birds. It is so cool and refreshing day. Farther down the way, he comes across a stream where he rolls his pants up and steps in the water. His feet slip on the rocks, and he has a difficult time walking, but he likes the cool water running around his ankles.

When he reaches the orchard, the old man is working with his spade in his new greenhouse. He is very happy to see his son.

"Ah ha, I see you have come to help me with the weeding. Over there I have a second spade."

"If you need my help, Father, I will be glad to help you."

"Come now. I cannot even joke with you? You have grown to such a man for what? Where are you off?"

"I am taking a stroll to the monastery, and I will be back at home for lunch."

"Alright, my son. God be with you."

Petros takes the road covered by trees and soon reaches the monastery. It is built on a rocky summit. A steep cliff leads all the way down to the sea, where the waves break gently. In the winter time this stronghold is beaten by the north winds and the rain. In the summer time it suffers from the burning heat. The monastery has a reputation among the locals because of the many miracles that have taken place here. An enemy cannonball is wedged in the wall of the sanctuary. It has been there for many years, and the monks claim that the grace of Mary the Virgin, whose name the church bares, stopped the ball, not allowing it to destroy her temple. As he passes through the entrance he finds himself in a large courtyard surrounded by the living quarters and storehouses. In the middle of the yard, with its back toward the east, stands the church.

Petros walks inside and lights a candle. A monk greets him warmly.

"Good morning, my child, which good wind brings you here?"

"Good morning, Father, I would like to ask the permission to look for something in the library of the monastery."

"Alright my child, come," says the monk looking at him a bit more intensely.

"Are you not Spathogeorge's son?"

"Yes, Father."

"How are your studies going?'

"Very well, Father."

He receives the prior's permission and walks over to the library, escorted by the monk.

"I am interested in the manuscripts, Father."

"Then look over that side, my child," The monk points to two large cases.

Petros opens them and starts searching. Soon he finds what he is looking for a two-centuries-old correspondence written in the old heavy dialect of the island. He reads eagerly and his glance freezes at one place.

> *... Occasionally, my brother, we have the opportunity to improve the living standards of our people. However, we do not succeed because we trust the diplomatic promises from the mainland. The revolution achieves nothing. We can succeed against the Turks, had the mainland government backed us ...*

It is written by a revolutionary from the island to a distant friend. The clear, intense, manly expression and the distinguished literary style of his ancestors impress Petros very much. He also finds the text amazingly suits life in Crete today. Indeed, if he wanted to write to a friend he would write exactly the same words today.

He reads enough from the correspondence until he is able to draw his own conclusion, which is necessary for him. His heart is calmed. After saying goodbye to the monk, he leaves. This time he changes his route and follows a narrow trail. He has to climb up a small hill in order to reach his village. Singing a local tune, he reaches the top of the hill and finds an old man on a donkey right ahead of him. He greets him and then asks,

"Are there any partridges around here, Uncle?"

"I have seen a couple of flocks over that mountain," the old man points to the other side of the horizon.

"Big flocks, I suppose, Uncle?"

"Yeah, big flocks," the old man nods with every word.

Petros gets a laugh at the old man's way of talking. They soon reach the village and say good-bye to each other.

He wants to help his father, but the old man won't let him; so the days go by in a relaxing manner, with him going to the beach once a day for a swim. His heart is at peace with everything around him. He goes on long strolls by himself in the orchards and along the hill by the village. Usually he sits on a high rock and gazes down at the plains with their gardens and melon fields. He looks around at the tranquil low hills and the abundant olive groves. His mind absorbs the harmonious bells from nearby goat herd; he inhales the fragrant breeze that wafts in from the sea. In such ideal moments of solitude, far from the world of the city, he feels himself throbbing with passion for the well being of the land and its peasants. He feels the spirit of the island surrounding him. This spirit, the same for centuries, is guiding him to his destiny, his destiny of serving his people on this island, and serving the people of whole Greece.

One day, his mother asks him whether he wants to go with his cousin to a baptism. He agrees. He likes the idea of attending such a celebration which he hasn't attended for a long time.

The next day at noon they start off traveling for almost two hours by bus to another village. The baptism ceremony takes place in a church and after that, they go to the boy's house for the celebration. When they arrive there they are guided to a long table in the garden underneath the grapevine arbor. The roasted lamb is placed in the middle of the table, and is surrounded by a variety of dishes—rice, salads, wine, bread, cheese pies, spinach pies, sweet pies, fruits—a big spread.

Everyone eats with a good appetite and drinks plenty of the wine. Petros feels as if he is back in time. He is a bit dizzy, but he keeps drinking along with the others every time someone proposes a toast.

Then the singing starts: "A thousand joys may come to the house of our friend . . ."

Then the host and his relatives answer in the same tune: "And a thousand welcomes to our friends in our home . . ."

What they continue to sing are the traditional songs: one person starts with a verse, all the rest repeat, then the first person starts a second verse and so on. This, of course, requires great attention as those who repeat should not make any mistake and carry further from where the first person stops. It is unforgivable to ruin the continuation of the song. But the people know this tradition well, and they continue for a long time. Two musicians arrive. They sit by the table for a short while, eat a few appetizers, drink a few glasses of wine, and then the dancing starts.

Petros' cousin Anthony is the one the villagers call Rifakas, and he is the best dancer of the area. He leads the guests in dancing. They begin with a fast *syrtos* that is characteristic of the area.

"To your health, Rifakas," the godfather calls out.

"And to yours," says Rifakas and turns to the musicians.

"Faster, for God's sake, faster, Stekonikolis faster; this tempo is for the old folk."

The lute player quickens the rhythm, and Rifakas dances, at times like a ram and at others like an eagle.

Now is the turn of the host and his relatives to take the lead. Their best is Vrochogeorgos, a man of great stature, who goes first. The rest of the family follows Vrochogeorgos and their goal is to show the first group that they can dance as well as they, or even better.

The vigor of youth is alive in these people in a very strong way. It is everywhere, in their words, in their ideas, in their open hearts. It is something that cannot be confined to their bodies; its abundance overflows, craving to scatter in the air, to defeat the laws of nature.

At times like that the sun shines and warms up the world, and the stormy sea becomes tranquil, changing to a purple color.

They eat and drink and dance without stopping for a long time. Later, the mood changes and they sing teasing verses back and forth to each other.

Petros feels so overwhelmed by the euphoria of the company that his pride arises again. The blood of the immortals that runs through his veins is the same blood that runs in the veins of these people, with their hairy chests and their large hands that can crush rocks.

The party winds down slowly as they approach early dawn. Petros' group boards the same bus that brought them here and return to their village.

Days go by, and he still cannot have enough of admiring this and that, observing ways of the locals, enjoying everything that comes along. Then one evening while Petros is at the café, his uncle calls from Athens, leaving him a message that the results from his exams are posted and the graduation ceremony is scheduled for two days later. Time has come for Petros to leave his village. He goes to town the next morning and reserves a ticket for the boat ride to Piraeus.

2

It is almost nightfall when the ship starts out with three loud whistles. The sky is clear, and the white reflection of the moon is mirrored in the sea, making it glow, creating a superb setting. The passengers, tired from daily hardships, anguish, and fatigue, rest on the seats and couches of the lounge. Their bodies smell of perspiration. Their minds relax, and their everyday problems are forgotten.

Petros thinks of the ceremony tomorrow afternoon to honor him and all the other graduates. This diploma means the end of his student life, and a new one is to unfold from here on with all its laughs and sorrows. The agony of all these years—the endless paper work, the essays, the hardships, the anxieties—is now coming to an end, and the reward is so close that he can almost smell it. He imagines how the faces of all the officials, the Dean, the Secretary, the Professors, and their assistants are going to reflect happiness, satisfaction, and pride. But then the things he has learned will begin to compete with his new life. He wants to work toward the betterment of the people who live under the regime which dictates all the rules. There may be no chance for anyone to stand opposite of the government unless his hide is ready for the burner or his bones for the crusher.

The ship has increased its speed, and hopefully will reach Piraeus early the next morning. The familiar hum of the engine is clearly heard, and the vibrations on the floor distinctly felt.

His mind returns to his mother as she saw him off at the bus terminal, his father bidding him farewell at the house before he left for his work. He wonders how many sleepless nights his mother and father must have gone through these past four years he has spent in

Athens under the care of his uncle and auntie. Many a time his parents were deeply worried about him because they did not understand where their son got all the ideas about changes needed in the society, in the country under the junta, and all that. Although he is his own man now (after all he is a graduate), still they are afraid of what may happen to him. Other times they think maybe they are just too old to understand the young generation.

Petros remembers his mother's blue eyes as he kissed her goodbye at the bus terminal. She looked at him with such a pride: this young man is her son, and all the nights she spent worrying about him were all worth it.

He closes his eyes and tries to sleep for a while since there is still a long way to go. The sound of the engine and the vibrations don't let him relax, though. He glances around at the rest of the passengers: many of them look ready to go to sleep, some read magazines, or newspapers, and two soldiers on the other side of the lounge are playing cards. His eyes are tired, sleepless, numb, and lazy. Luckily, he does not have to share this small couch. His legs feel a bit more relaxed as he stretches them and gets into a comfortable position. Then he picks up a magazine from the side table and tries to read. He flips through the pages, but his mind cannot concentrate as it is attracted to someplace else: imperceptible things and indeterminate events. Suddenly a strange shudder runs through his body.

Then, quite unexpectedly, sleep takes control of his eyes. He wakes up later when the day breaks. His watch says eight a.m.; he is almost at his destination. There is no wind outside, the sea is calm, and the ship rolls gently on the froth of the small waves.

The ticket collector, a man with long sideburns, comes by. Petros asks him what time they are to arrive, and the man answers that they are to dock within the hour. He then goes to the coffee bar to get his morning coffee. No one else is at the bar; they must be busy packing their things and getting ready to disembark. The waiter behind the bar whistles as he cleans up. Petros smiles at him who reciprocates and carries on what he is doing.

The ship whistles as it docks, and the doors are opened. The passengers rush out like a swarm of bats flying out of their hiding place.

Petros grabs his small suitcase and heads toward the exit staircase. There is a large crowd outside, people of all ages and all kinds. As soon as they recognize a familiar face, they greet and kiss one another on the cheek, laughing and making jokes.

Crowds of people move around like swarms of bees, living the sadness of the days without sign of regret or animosity. Most of those people are bone skinny, and a few puffed up like donuts, with their stomachs filled and their favored cigars lit, not affected at all by the sad condition of the majority. Women as well are in different castes: most are ordinary-looking housewives of the gossip circle, and of course a few are the ones usually found in the aristocratic bars and lounges, ladies with housemaids and black chauffeurs, with small bedroom dogs and a gigolo on the side. Petros always looks down on the so-called upper class; a degrading and pathetic life, he thinks they are like snakes. Those people have all the money they need, with their luxurious cars and drug addictions or similar kinds of crap, and they blindly follow whatever is "modern," a certain mania to do as the foreigners do, to just be part of something trendy. According to Petros, this way of living does nothing to improve a person's life. He doesn't belong to the idealists and skeptics, either, who ignore reality and live in the clouds of their isolation with the hope that the world will change on its own volition on some fine morning and everything will just be splendid. What he wants is a major change in society, a change that makes the commoners' lives better and the upper class more decent and more confidant people. A smile comes to his face as if he has already been affected by such a change.

He walks as he disembarks the ship. His uncle, Demetre, is amongst the others on the dock, lordly as always, waving his hand. Petros beams a big smile and walks to him.

"Welcome, my boy, how was your trip?" his uncle puts his arm around Petros' shoulder, a gesture he uses rarely.

"It was fine, Uncle."

"Congratulations, and on to greater things!"

"Thank you, Uncle, thank you very much. How is my aunt doing?"

"She is very well, thank you, all excited as you can understand."

Demetre is quite pleased with his nephew and the forthcoming diploma. He is the first to see the posted results; something even Petros hasn't done yet. They walk to the car parked nearby, and Demetre drives away.

Demetre is a semi-retired bureaucrat who has about ten other nieces and nephews from his wife's side, yet Petros is his favorite, although he rarely shows his feelings to Petros, unlike his wife who is always expressive and appreciative for all the efforts made by this young nephew who has dreams to reach the stars. When Demetre decides to reveal his emotion, he becomes a completely different person: he drops the serious look on his face, leaves the formalities aside, and comes alive. He has never had any children, and this nephew is as close as a son gets. He sees in the face of this young man his own dreams of going to university and getting the education he'd love to have had when he was young.

They arrive at home, an elegant and spacious house of neoclassic design, with its enormous yard, lawn, garden, and garage. Not many houses in this city have a garage at this time of history. There is also a small pavilion toward the end of the garden. Petros has spent plenty of time there studying or simply daydreaming, an occupation he's very good at.

He remembers how he often sat in the pavilion all night while the crickets kept him company with their songs. He used to find his world there, and most of the times his inner self. There, he could think freely without the noise of the city, there, he could make his plans about what to do when his time comes to become an adult in the society, and there, he could find answers to all the difficult questions every time.

They enter the house. His aunt, Maria, smiling and cheerful as always, embraces Petros and holds on to him for a moment. She cannot conceal her pride and love for this young man.

"Congratulations, my boy, I am so happy for you."

"Thank you, my dear aunt."

Happy tears appear in her eyes. This woman whom Petros always admires for her strength simply cannot control her emotions. There is nothing her husband or Petros can do about it.

Maria is a tall, skinny, graceful woman who never had any children. In Petros she sees her son, the one she wished she had. Her large forehead, her black eyes, her delicate nose, her thin lips, her whole face—are in Petros, reflecting a happiness and sadness for the son they never had.

"At 11:30 you must be at school, my son, to take your oath, and at noon the ceremony will take place with the diplomas. You have enough time to rest for a bit and prepare yourself," Maria says.

"Very well then, I might as well start doing something." Petros takes his suitcase and goes upstairs to his room.

The bed is still covered with the same familiar blue blanket. His bureau, his desk, his books are all there. This is the world where he has spent the last four years of his life. He is surrounded again with the familiar setting and all the love he easily feels and even tastes. He lies on the bed and lets his thoughts flow. A few minutes later, a knock on the door announces his auntie with a tray of breakfast. For so many years she has taken care of him and spoiled him with adoration. She leaves the tray on the bureau, bends down to kiss his forehead, and then goes out, closing the door behind her.

He arrives at the school later in the day after he meets with Eleni at their usual spot to catch the bus together. Upon arrival, they make their way toward the second floor where the oath will take place. In the hall he is stopped to sign the register.

"Well, well, let's welcome the philosopher."

He turns and sees some of his classmates, along with his buddy Pavlos.

"Hi there, how are you guys doing?"

"Just fine," one of the men says, "but we started to believe you wouldn't make it on time. As always, you are the last."

"Last but not least," a female classmate says with a smile.

Pavlos puts his arm around Petros' shoulders.

"Well, man, we made it. This is the day."

"I know. Who can believe it, eh?" Petros laughs and then notices something: "What is happening? Everything around here seems so different today. Do you see it, or is it just me?"

"Nothing is changed, my friend. It is just that in a while we are going out of here for good. You know what that means?"

One of the clerks from the secretary's office interrupts, "Follow me, please." She guides them to a classroom. They take their seats, as do the guests, and one by one the professors come in and take their seats as well. The dean walks in at the last with a big smile. He greets them all and sits in his chair. At last everything is ready. Then Petros hears the secretary calling his name. He gets up, approaches the secretary, and takes from her hand an envelope that contains the official legal oath. Complete silence prevails in the room. He slowly and carefully reads the oath and at the end of the text all his classmates repeat unanimously:

"I swear."

Then the congratulations begin. One by one the graduates walk by the dean, who shakes their hands and wishes them the best future. Then the dean gives his speech, and as always, predicts that these young graduates are going to be more successful than the previous class. Those are the same words Petros Spathis and the others have heard before. It seems that the dean has learned this speech by heart, reciting it like a parrot, no matter what is the country's current situation.

Petros sits next to Eleni, feeling bored and angry: under the junta, things are not going to be better and the graduates are not going to do better than the previous ones. If nothing is done, things are only going to get worse. He has to try very hard to be attentive, and when his name is called, he gets up and walks slowly to the dean, who smiles and shakes his hand before handing him the "holy" paper. Petros nods his head and smiles politely at the dean and the rest of the officials, as well as his professors. Inside, Petros feels the urge to stand up in front of them all and give them a real piece of his mind, but he knows it's not his time yet, so he goes back to his seat. His head throbs from the tension. Eleni senses that he is absorbed to his own world and asks, "Are you okay? You look like you don't like being here."

"I have this bad headache. My head is really hurting."

"This thing is just about over. We'll go soon."

He nods, and indeed the ceremony is quickly over, and the people start to disperse. He and Eleni rise from their seats and walk toward the exit.

At the door, George, a clerk from the secretary's office, stops them.

"Again congratulations, young man."

"Oh, thank you, George."

"The dean would like to see you before you go."

Surprised, Petros leaves Eleni and follows the long hallway to the dean's office. He knocks at the door and enters. The head of the university welcomes him and praises him for all the good work he has done. After all, Petros is the student with the highest marks and that is the reason why he was the one who read the oath document. Petros waits for the dean to go to the point.

"Spathis, I am in the delightful position to tell you that we would like to offer you the chair of economics. The school has carefully followed your achievements from the first year to the last, and we received permission from the Ministry of Education. Therefore, I welcome you in this university as a colleague." He extends his hand to Petros.

He is speechless. He never expected them to offer him such a position right after his graduation. Now his head is really throbbing. He doesn't know what to say. He shakes the dean's hand and utters, "Oh, thank you very much, Dean. What an unexpected surprise, but a very pleasant one may I add. I am overwhelmed. Is it possible for me to postpone the decision for another day?"

"Of course, you can take your time. This position is open for you, only for you, for a while. How about you come by my house tomorrow or the next day and we can chat about it. Besides, there are a few other things you need to consider since it is imperative that you go abroad for two years to take up studies before you can really establish yourself completely at this post. However, everything has being taken care of: the scholarship, the financial aspects, everything."

"The day after tomorrow sounds the best to me, Dean. I'll come by your residence for sure."

"Great. I look forward to seeing you. Good day, Spathis."

"Good day, Dean."

Petros hurries out and finds Eleni with Pavlos and a couple of other graduates who are curious about what happened. However, he is in no mood for a long discussion, so he only gives them the gist. They are happy for him and urge him to accept. Petros tells them that he needs to think about it, and takes Eleni by the arm and they leave. They take the bus and go to Eleni's house. Her parents have been away for a month, and now the house is just for the two lovers. When they get inside, she hugs and kisses him passionately. His mind becomes preoccupied by the heat of her body, and they make passionate love.

The extreme cool days of the previous month are a contrast to the warm weather they have had these last days. Clouds appear here and there just enough to tell people that winter hasn't gone yet. Some trees have started the annual change with the first sign of buds. Migratory birds have mostly arrived from their journey, starting in the tropical climates of Northern Africa. In the countryside the farmers are organizing the fields for the early summer vegetables and fruits. All the fields of tomatoes, cucumbers, melons have to be cleared of all the weeds and get fertilized, and the water supply line has to be put in place. There is so much work to do and Petros' father has his share of all that, especially this year with his new greenhouse in place.

Petros has been busy with his thoughts of what to do with the dean's offer. Two days have gone by. He knows his uncle and aunt will understand, and whatever his decision may be, they will accept it with pleasure. Yet, he has to consider the position of his parents if he has to go abroad for a while. He doesn't like the idea of hurting them in any way, but this is his chance to get in a place from where he can create changes to the things he would like to see, to the things he has been dreaming of all his life. Then there is Eleni: he loves this girl and he doesn't want to let her go. However, she has implied her desire for a more solid relationship, and he knows that she means marriage. Petros is not ready for a promise of this kind, no matter if it takes place much later. Now with this opportunity in front of him, she is a bit uptight, as she doesn't like him to be away from her for so long.

He is in his room with his mind wondering to far-away lands where he may have to go for a while. Yes, he has to accept the offer. This position is going to be his post. Even if he has to go abroad, it's going to be just for a while. He likes the idea of being around the young people who can be molded to his way of thinking. He will be a craftsman who takes soil and plants it into a pot of his liking. Yes, this is a position he has to accept.

"Everything will go the way it is supposed to go," Petros tells himself. Cleaned and dressed, he goes downstairs. His aunt is there.

"Ready to go, my boy?"

"Yes, dear Aunt. I shouldn't be late."

"You are right. Go then and try to learn everything, so you know what you will get yourself into, conditions, demands, everything, okay? Remember nobody these days offers you something without expecting something in return."

"Yes, I know, I will find out the best I can. Don't worry. I'll tell you all about it when I'm back."

"Are you going to be late?"

"No, and I'm not going to Eleni's after this, if that's what you are saying," he answers and goes to the door.

Half an hour later he is at the doorstep of the dean's house and rings the bell. The dean himself opens the door.

"Good evening, Dean."

"Good evening, Spathis. Come in."

He walks in and sits down in an arm chair. The house is rich, lordly, with thick carpets and furniture of a conservative style. All kinds of paintings hang on the walls. The smiling dean sits across from him.

"Would you like to have a drink?"

"Thank you Dean, a coffee will be great."

The dean's wife walks in, greets Petros politely, asks what he would like in his coffee, and discreetly leaves them alone.

"Well, Spathis, I would like to get directly to the point, so let me start by asking how you like this offer from the school. It is a great position for a young man, don't you think?"

"Once again, Dean, I would like to thank you. Yes, indeed, it is an excellent position, and I am quite inclined to say yes to you, although I still need to know a few more details before I make my decision."

He is quite clear in his words, and the head of the school likes that.

"I see with pleasure that you like to walk on steady ground, Spathis, I couldn't expect anything less than that; it is a bold move if you accept this," the dean says as his wife comes in with the coffee.

"I hope it is to your liking," the wife says after serving Petros.

"I'm sure it is, Madam. Thank you."

She walks out, and the dean carries on with their conversation.

"Things will unfold like this, Spathis. You need to go abroad and specialize in a subject for two years. The assistant of the previous professor currently occupies the chair of economics, and we look forward to having a new professor there."

"You have talked to the Minister of Education, Dean?"

"Of course, and I have mentioned to him that I consider you the best for this position right now."

"Thank you so much, Dean. You mentioned last time that you have also taken care of my expenses for two years of studies abroad. Can you tell me more about it?"

"Don't worry about the financial part of this, Spathis. I have looked into every detail. The scholarship funds will be enough to cover your studies, including the accommodation and food. Now, for personal expenses, of course, you have to look into it yourself. I hope you can find a way. Keep me informed on this since I don't mind at all to secure some more money personally and make it available to you if needed. Just remember, Spathis, I would like you to come back ready to take this position and work with me in this university. I see in you a scholar who will reach the top of the ladder very soon. If by some chance I am not in my position to help you by the time you return, you will work with a colleague of mine. One doesn't know how to look at things these days because of the country's political situation, you understand."

The dean gets up and walks to the bar to pour a drink. He smiles as he remembers the minister telling him that no matter what it takes, he'd better succeed in convincing this young man. A younger man like Petros in such a position would be easier to work with since he carries no "baggage," as it is in most cases with academia these days, and the junta likes things in a simple, clear-cut way. Petros feels guilty over his earlier hesitation.

"Truly, Dean, I do not know how to say no, since you have gone to so much trouble to put all this together for me. I cannot disappoint you, I am very happy to accept this position, and I look forward to working with you when I'm back. Regarding the financial subject, it is not necessary for you to find more money for me because I'm sure I can take care of my personal expenses. On the other hand, I'd like to state one or two conditions of my own in this matter. Although it is very early to worry about this, I would like to have your understanding that when I am working in this university, I do not want to have anyone on my head. I want to have freedom of movement and no condition attached from the current politicos. I do not want to have restrictions imposed upon my job by anyone in the political system. This is a personal matter, and I insist on it."

The dean smiles, "I understand quite clearly what you like to have, Spathis, and I agree, although it is still too early to discuss such a matter. Let us leave this subject for the time being."

"Alright, Dean."

Petros notices that his demand caused a reaction from the dean even though the dean tried to conceal it. However, he feels that such a subject should be discussed ahead of time. Honesty leads to solid friendship. That is what Petros always believes.

"Now it is my turn to ask of a favor of you, Spathis."

"No problem, Dean."

"The country we are talking about is Canada. McGill University and University of British Columbia are the two we recommend, and which I have personally contacted. If you can get a positive response from either of the two, and Canada is where you would like to go, I'd like you to do a short research project for me about their stock exchange system, with as many details as possible about their operations and regulations, federal or provincial. I am looking into ways of applying similar things here in our stock exchange."

"Of course, Dean. When I'm there, I'll make sure I get this information for you. I have also noticed that many areas in our school and society need to improve."

"I'm aware of that too, Spathis. Now, you see, these are examples of how you can make so much difference in the way things are done here. Another reason why I recommended you to the minister is that I can see the wisdom in your words, and I'm sure we are going to have an excellent working relationship when you come back."

"I look forward to that, Dean. Perhaps we may be able to affect some good changes to help all our countrymen."

"Now, now, Spathis, we don't want to go too far for now, do we?"

"I guess you are right, Dean. We'd better leave the subject of the political situation for some other day. I do strongly believe that the changes have to start from the top . . ."

The dean turns and looks at the other side of the room before he clears his throat and comments, "Spathis don't forget to get into the details of the applications and all the rest. Keep me posted with whatever happens."

"Yes, Dean, I'll look after it as early as tomorrow."

He gets up and says good night to both the dean and his wife. A divine feeling of optimism comes over him, a feeling of satisfaction and joy, and it is clear like the cloudless sky.

3

He jumps from his bed eagerly at the crack of dawn and stands by the window looking outside below his bedroom. His insatiable glance in a split second moves across the horizon to embrace the whole world. It is raining lightly, and the water drips from the tree branches into the garden. A small sparrow flutters in between the branches of the shrubs. It darts in and out among the leaves, flapping its wings as if receiving the rain with pleasure.

Petros Spathis' mind flies along with the sparrow: "How wonderful nature is! The female being, the earth, receiving with joy the manly rain, is satisfied. Is it a chain and a circle? Or is it a circle and a chain?"

He takes a shower, feeling like a different man. When he comes downstairs for breakfast, his aunt and uncle are waiting for him.

"Good morning."

"Good morning, my son, did you sleep well?" his auntie asks.

"Yes, I slept well, dear Aunt."

He takes his glass of milk and drinks it all in one breath. Then, he takes a piece of toast and spreads some marmalade on it. This usually goes well with his coffee.

His uncle, eager to find out what his nephew's decision is, starts with a question: "Well, what are you thinking of doing, Son?"

Petros takes a deep breath, needing the time to think before he answers,

"I like the dean's offer, I believe it is going to be quite a job and I should take this opportunity. Of course there is the fact that I have to go abroad for a couple of years, but that is the way the cookie crumbles, as the saying goes. I cannot avoid that: it is part of the package. When I return, I will be hired, no questions asked. The dean assured me of this a few times. Of course I need to talk to my parents, who I'm sure won't like the idea of two years in a foreign country. I would like to hear your opinion though. From both of you. You two have been my second parents for so long, and you understand this a bit more than my father and my mother."

His aunt sits there, silently looking at him with great affection, this child who makes her feel so proud.

Demetre clears his throat and starts, "This definitely is a very good offer, a position which many others would love to have. It's a lot better than being hired as a clerk at some bank or a government position, although that would be perhaps a steadier career. Still, this is better for you because it will open quite a wide field of action for you at a later time. Of course, the disadvantage is that you need to go away for a while. It is, after all, a serious thing to go so far and be a stranger amongst strangers, with no friends, and all that. On the other hand, if that is what it takes, that is what a man does."

Petros smiles at the last piece of his uncle's comment,

"Yes, there is always a way where there is a will. I believe in what I can do, and I know deep inside that after the hardship, I'm going to be where I like to be and amongst the people I like the most."

"We know you well," his uncle says, "and we know that we cannot go against what you want to do. Besides, you are in many ways exceptional, and you owe it to yourself to achieve great success."

Demetre is right: he sees in this young man the soul of the eagle living near the mountain peaks, unconquered by time. He will remind him of this at every step of his way. Petros realizes clearly now it is his duty to try, and it is his duty not to fail, although the word fail is one he never has in his vocabulary. He knows clearly now that he owes this to his destiny, because it is no less than that of his holy ancestors whose lives were filled with greatness and those attempts toward greatness. If he ever falls, Petros Spathis wants to fall from so high up that even the fall will have its own greatness.

"Talk to your parents, and then we'll discuss this again, but I must also caution you that you may need to get a part-time job over there while you take your courses, and of course that may delay your return, so we have decided that we'll give you what we think is necessary, so you won't need to worry about work and can concentrate on your studies. We want you to finish as soon as possible. Of course, we'd like you to forget about talking to my brother and your mother about this. You know my brother is a very proud man, and he is probably going to make a fuss if he knows about this."

Petros feels a big lump form in his throat. He doesn't know what else to say to these two lovely people. He has so much gratitude and respect for them.

"Oh, I thank you both so much. I don't think I will need much more than what the scholarship will provide for me. When I'm there, I promise to let you know, and you can do as you please."

"Oh, no, there is no need for that," Demetre says, "I'll post a certain amount of money every month, and if it happens that you don't spend it all, no need to send it back here. Send it to your parents: you know your father is a very proud man who would never accept anything from me, even if he needs it." His uncle suddenly sighs, "I wish I could get the chance to go and see my brother, if I didn't have this business to attend to. I haven't seen him for more than three years." His expression changes with nostalgia.

Maria interrupts,

"Why don't you go, Demetre? The employees can be without you in the office for a few days. Go and see your brother; we only get older everyday. Go. You never know what my happen. George will love to see you again."

Her voice is so convincing that Demetre doesn't need any more encouragement. Excited, he gets up as if he needed to get ready right at this moment, and then he pauses and says, "You are right, my dear. By the way, Son, what time is the flight?"

"Six in the evening, Uncle."

"Alright then, when you go to get the tickets, get two instead of one. We shall go together."

"Very well then, I'll do that. It will also give us the chance to go hunting again like the old days."

Demetre then leaves to meet his friend for their daily walk in the park. They live in the northern suburbs of Athens, and there are many trees here and there. Petros stays with his aunt for a while. She likes to talk to him about a girl, yet she finds it hard to start a conversation about her since she knows he is quite attracted to Eleni. However, her good friend Mrs Avgeriou has been asking her lately whether there is a chance for her daughter Magda to get acquainted with Petros—after all, he is a handsome young man whom Magda is very fond of.

"Petros, my son, I have to ask you . . . something . . ." Maria's words do not come out freely.

He senses that he has to give her his help: "What is it my aunt? Please tell me."

"You remember Magda Avgeriou? You met her here a few months ago when we had your uncle's name day party?"

He hesitates for a while, and yes, he remembers a good-looking girl. His aunt made sure to introduce her to him.

"Yes, I remember her, the tall girl with short hair."

"Yes, that is her. Do you like her? I mean, how do you like to get to know her better?"

"Why, are you proposing that I meet this girl intimately, my aunt?"

She pulls back for a second.

"God, no, I don't mean that. Her mother has asked a few times lately if you may be interested in going out with Magda. You know how things are done sometimes, my son. A mother is always on a look out for a good young man for her daughter. I don't totally disagree with her."

He smiles and gives her a kiss on the cheek.

"Sorry, my dear aunt. I don't think I can go out with Magda right now. You know I like Eleni very much. I'd rather not give any false hopes to Magda and then walk away when the time comes. You know, now that you have mentioned this matter, I want to tell you that I'm not really ready to commit myself to anybody, even to Eleni, although I sense her wish for a more definite relationship. I am just not ready for a marriage."

"But why, my son, you have finished your studies, you have finished your army duties; after two years abroad you will come back, and then you can settle down. Every young man comes to this point in life when they start a family. Magda, and Eleni for that matter, are two very pretty young women. What stops you from seeing them as wives?"

"Yes, I know they are pretty, and Magda comes from a very rich family, and of course her parents are your friends, but my first priority at this time is my schooling. When I'm finished and return here, I'll have to decide what to do about my responsibility to society and other things. But I thank you for doing this for me, my dear aunt, and I promise that you will be the first one to know when the time comes."

She smiles and hugs him.

"I know my son, thank you. Don't forget this girl comes from a good family and a good circle of people. They have very good connections all over Athens. You never know, some day you may find them helpful when you are in trouble. Magda likes you, and I'm sure she would love to be in touch with you when you are abroad. Why don't you try to keep in touch with her? I ask you this as a favor."

He is cornered, and he hates the idea of disappointing her.

"Well, if that is going to make you happy, I may keep in touch with her when I'm abroad. But of course you realize and she should know that I intend to be in touch with Eleni as well."

"Very well then, that is settled. I'll talk to her mother."

He laughs.

"You do as you please. On the other hand, I'll call Magda to make sure I see her when I'm back from Crete. How does that sound?"

She is very happy to hear that.

"Yes that sounds excellent, my son. Let me go now and start preparing our meal before it gets too late; when Demetre returns home, he likes to eat his lunch right away. Come to think of it, why don't you talk to your mom and dad about Magda?"

"No, no, that can't be done. If I tell them this, their answer will be to marry the girl right away and don't leave. When they hear about a good family and money, they will not listen to reason."

His aunt doesn't want to pressure him anymore because she knows her husband will also talk to him on their way to Crete.

Petros leaves to get the tickets for their flight. He meets with Eleni on their usual spot, and they take the bus together to Syntagma Square, where the Olympic Airlines have one of their offices. Eleni is silent for most of the ride, and he senses why. She knows the time will eventually come when he is gone to this far-away place, and she knows that when he is there he will be on his own, far from her and her eyes. There are so many dangers and distractions for a man of his age. There are so many pretty girls abroad: she has seen them in the theaters and on television. He may never come back to her.

"Hey, you haven't said anything for a while. Is everything okay?"

"Yes, everything is okay."

"Why all the silence then?"

"I'm afraid. I'm scared of you going so far away and for such a long time."

She mentioned this before, and he can see it in her eyes every time. Yet there is no way he can give up this opportunity. Eleni simply has to understand this and sit back and wait.

"Don't be. Two years is not the end of the world. I'll be back so soon you won't even feel it."

They arrive at Syntagma Square, which is quite crowded with shoppers. Petros and Eleni make their way slowly, holding hands and walk across the plaza to the airline office. Parents and their children play in the middle of the square, and as Petros and Eleni pass by, a ball rolls toward them. Petros picks it up and gives it to the young little boy who was running after it. When the boy grimaces at them instead of saying thank you, Petros says, "Little rascal." Both Eleni and Petros laugh.

"Yeah, not even a simple thank you," she agrees.

They reach the office, where Petros buys two tickets. She turns and asks,

"How long are you going to stay this time?"

"Just for a few days, perhaps a week. I'll be back sooner than you think. Where would you like to go now?"

She says nothing, taking his hand and starting back toward the bus stop. When they get inside her parent's house, she doesn't even care to look around for any of the neighbors who may be peeping, and before long they are completely naked. She is so hungry for him that she leans down and takes him in her mouth. He lies back and lets her do as she pleases, and he does the same when she decides to ride on top of him. He closes his eyes and enjoys all her effort; her breasts bounce up and down as she reaches her orgasm, which comes once then twice. He loves the sight of her breasts moving; her sexuality has been a very serious bond between them.

They lay down, exhausted, and she lights a cigarette, which he always complains about. He takes the cigarette out of her mouth and puts it out in the ashtray, to her obvious disappointment. Then he turns her around and enters her from behind, something he enjoys the most.

Later he rises from the bed and gets ready to leave. She becomes upset again and hugs him as if she would never see him again.

"I'll be back before you even notice."

"Promise to call me."

"I will, although you know the phone service from the village is not the best. I'll call you tomorrow, I promise."

Back at his uncle's house, Demetre and Maria are waiting for him to come home. Maria keeps looking at the wall clock.

Demetre asks, "Did you get a chance to talk to him about Magda?"

"Yes, I told him, but I don't know. He seems to be involved with this Eleni a lot more than what we think. I don't know what else to say. He did promise to go out with Magda when you two come back from Crete."

"Well, that's a good piece of news, I'd say. Perhaps I should tell my brother."

"No, don't say anything. I mentioned that to him, and he was alarmed and said if his parents knew about this girl, they would like him to forego his trip. That is something he doesn't want to hear at all."

Their discussion is interrupted when they hear Petros' footsteps. They have wide smiles to welcome him home.

"Got them?" Demetre asks.

"Yes, Uncle, we fly at six-fifteen. We should start from here around four. It takes a bit less than an hour to get to the airport."

"Yes, that sounds just fine."

Petros goes to his room to organize his small bag; Maria has prepared Demetre's already.

"Make sure you send my greetings to your family, my son," his aunt says as they get into the taxi.

It is a half-clear day, with a few clouds here and there in the sky. They board a small jet with two motors. The thirty-minute air flight is a bit bumpy, and then they arrive to the Chania airport on time. After landing, they ride the airline bus to the center of Chania, where they find a cab to take them to the village, a drive about half an hour long.

They travel in silence, tired. Demetre can't find a way to take him away from his thoughts. He would like to talk to Petros about Magda. But the young man is in a melancholic mood, just like the overcast sky over them and the monotonous light rain of Crete.

Petros Spathis feels heaviness on his chest. When arriving at his parents' house, he will show them the graduating papers which are resting inside his small briefcase that he also brought with him. He wants them to feel pride for his diploma, something many people would love to have. Yet he has this unbearable weight on his heart, and he can see it with the eyes of his soul, a soul big enough to take in the whole world, the world with poverty and diseases, with its wars and disasters, and with its love and virtue, with its sunshine and rain, the same rain outside the car which is taking them home.

His uncle breaks the silence first.

"Your aunt, did she tell you something about Magda?"

"Yes, she did, Uncle. What about her?"

"She is an exceptional girl: beautiful and educated with social graces. She also comes from a very rich family, and her father has many significant ties to the industrial world, to government circles, you name it. You should think about this partnership very seriously. Besides, I think she is in love with you; she always talks about you and would love to go out with you. I know, of course, that you are dating Eleni, but Madga is a different girl: she has everything a man would ask for. Don't forget that good connections are very important these days, just as they have been all along."

Petros listens to him carefully, weighing every word that his uncle says before taking his turn: "What concern me most are this job offer and my career. First I'll have to take care of all these, and when I return from abroad, I'm going to do some thinking regarding a marriage. You shouldn't have referred to the fact that her father's connections are going to help because you know me, and you know how I feel about that. If I don't feel that I fit in a certain place, her father won't make it happen even if he wants to."

Demetre bites his lip, knowing that he has upturned a very heavy rock with his words, and he tries to change the subject: "I leave it with you then. I won't say anything anymore until you come back from your studies. I only insist that you think about it."

Their discussion stops, and they notice that the village has come into view. The village lies along the slope of a hill, the white houses in the distance shining from rain, which has just stopped. The larger homes are two story's tall, like castles of older times. The rest are one-level, but all are built the same way, as though a supernatural force, erupting from the ground and the rocks of the hill, raised them up. There are no trees in sight, only stones and boulders. They now are getting closer to the village's one hundred cottages that are inhabited by three- or four-hundred hardy souls. Below the village is the valley, with running waters for irrigation. The villagers are of two different castes: one of the fields and the other of the mountains. The patriarch of each family owns a part of the land in the valley and its water, a piece of Earth which he takes good care of, and in which he plants the best seed and uses the best fertilizer. The only village complaint is about the water: there is never enough—just as their luck is not enough—thus, the water is always the subject for arguments and fights.

"Ah, my poor village," sighs Demetre as they near. It is as though he comes here for the first time in his life.

"Uncle, has it really been three years since you were here last?"

"Yes, exactly, and you cannot imagine how much I have longed to return."

The car enters the village square that is surrounded by houses and two coffee shops. A group of children with red cheeks and bright eyes gather around the car, closely examining it with admiration. Most of them wear hoods and galoshes. The square is full of puddles, and all day long the children splash and play in them.

The first impressions, the first greetings, and the sweet feeling of being reunited after all this time overwhelm Demetre, although not so much for Petros, who was here not that long ago. At the coffee bar, the people who know them and even the ones who don't welcome them, with evident joy, and ask them to sit down to have a glass of brandy. The mayor of the village is also there to welcome them, and makes an official announcement of their welcome. The mayor is a high school graduate, a fact that puts him higher up on the social scale than others, since most people at this time of history didn't go to high school, giving up their studies to work in the fields and to herd the goats and sheep in the mountains. Yet the mayor knows how to write and read well; he can write without being embarrassed about his spelling, vocabulary, or grammar; he even writes his own speeches. The man speaks with Petros and Demetre, asking how they live in the city. Then he, in turn, tells them about the village news, the fields, the sowing, the planting, the harvesting, and the profit each of the villagers makes.

"I see that you use greenhouses for the vegetables," Demetre comments. "It is a very good method and will bring bigger profits, isn't that right?"

"Yes, of course," the mayor says. "The idea for the greenhouses was mine, and then everybody soon followed," he adds proudly.

People crowd around, tuning their ears to their conversation. "Where is my brother?" Demetre asks.

"He must be out in his field." says the head of the village. "He always works there."

Petros turns to his uncle.

"Shall we go home now, Uncle?"

"Come now, young Spathis, stay for a while," the mayor insists. "It's not often that we get the chance to talk to an educated man from the city. I hear you have finished your schooling. Do you have your diploma?"

"Well yes, Mayor. I have graduated and received my degree."

"Well done, Petros, congratulations! This calls for another brandy." He turns to the waiter and gives the order: "Foti, a glass of brandy for everyone, my treat. Let us all celebrate for the success of Petros Spathis and wish him all the best in the future."

So they all take a drink to the young man's success and wish him many better things in the future.

"Thank you all very much. Really. You make this day a very pleasant one. However, I have to go because I'm impatient to see my mother."

The mayor agrees with that, yet he doesn't want them to go yet.

"Well, let us see this diploma of yours."

Petros cannot resist that request, so he opens his briefcase, takes out his diploma, and gives it to the mayor whose hands tremble when he takes it in as though he were touching the Bible. The mayor examines it with great curiosity while fellow villagers look over his shoulder to get a good look at this piece of paper, too.

"So this is a diploma," says the envious mayor when he hands it back to Petros.

"Yes, this is the diploma and here is my award." Petros shows him another piece of paper with golden letters and official stamps honoring him for his excellent standings in the class.

"You also received an award, Petros?" the mayor's eyes widen. "Bravo! My congratulations once again!"

He looks at the paper more closely and asks.

"So what are you going to do now, young Spathis? Become an economist? What does an economist do?"

Petros gives them a brief explanation of what an economist is and how he has a scholarship for studying abroad for two years and then will be teaching at the university. The mayor and the others have a hard time understanding what all these mean.

"Scholarship to go to another country and study," the mayor says. "Which country you heading for?"

"Canada."

The crowd turns to look at one another with awe on their faces. They feel quite proud for the son of George Spathis; not too many young men from the area get the chance to go to the city and study, never mind accomplishing what Petros has, this far, this fast. Demetre is truly proud of this young man who has brought their family and ancestors this honor of achievement.

Smiling, Demetre takes Petros away from the crowds.

"Time for us to go to my brother's place."

So they say their goodbyes and start their walk to the house at the other end of the village. They follow a narrow lane, and in a few minutes arrive at the house. As they approach his father's dog, the hound, starts to bark. The uncle and his nephew are not even inside the fence when his mother, as though by instinct, comes out of the house and sees them.

"My son!" she hugs Petros. She holds him for a good minute and then remembers that he arrived with Demetre. "Hello Demetre, welcome. How is Maria with her health?"

"She is good, you know. As we age, everything seems in need for some repair, here and there." Demetre tells her.

"When is my father coming home, Mother?"

"It should be anytime now, my son. Now what can I serve you? After this trip, you both should be hungry."

Petros tells his mother to sit down so they can chat for a while first, and later they will eat when his dad comes and joins them.

It is not long before they hear George's footsteps from the yard. Then his father appears, tall, arrogant, blonde with blue eyes, his straight hair combed back, dressed in old working clothes, covered with dust, and holding a bag full of vegetables.

"Well, well, welcome," he goes cheerfully and hugs his brother. "I see you finally remember we live here. What happened to you? We haven't seen you for three years, how is Maria?"

"Maria is just fine, George. I see as time goes by you are growing younger. Rumor has it you started a business," Demetre jokes with him.

"Hey, not a business, really. It's only a greenhouse in which I'm going to plant for the first time this year . . . the summer vegetables, you know, the tomatoes, cucumbers, things like that; and I intend to grow the best fall and winter vegetables later on."

The mother who stands there holding her son's diploma and award interrupts them impatiently,

"George, here are our son's papers: his diploma and his award. He was first in the class, I will have you know."

George is overwhelmed by the news. Feeling so proud for his son, he gives Petros a big hug, something he has never done before, as far as Petros can recall.

"You received an award as well?" he asks loudly as if to make sure he has heard his wife properly.

"Yes, Father," says Petros, "but I have something else I need to tell you and Mother. I need to go to Canada to study for a while. This is going to give me the opportunity to accept a good position they offered me at the university."

His parents freeze. Then his mother raises her voice in fear: "You need to go to Canada? What are you going to do there alone? Who is going to take care of you? Who is going to clean your clothes? Who is going to cook for you?"

She sees her son as a little boy still, and wonders how he can survive without relatives around to help him.

George is silent, and after a while he utters a few more questions: "Why don't you forget about going abroad and get a different job, someplace else? What happens if you don't go?"

Demetre interrupts, "Yes, he can find a job in one of the government agencies, or he can become a civil servant or have a position in a bank, things like that. If he goes abroad for a while and comes back, he is guaranteed a professorship at the same university he graduated from. It's a much better job, much more respected."

George still wants to find some other reasons to have Petros give up the idea of the foreign country, something that doesn't go well in his mind.

"What about the expense for such a trip? How are we going to find the money to pay for this?"

Demetre steps in again, "Your son needs to go away for a while to specialize in a field study. Then, when he returns he will become a professor at the university. It is a very good job, a very powerful one. But without going abroad to do his special studies, he can't qualify for the position. But don't worry, we will not have to pay anything for it, not a penny; the government has given him a scholarship for this."

George still insists, "Can he not find a good job without the trip?"

Petros now feels that he has to say something:

"Mother, Father, thank you for your input, but it is for my future and, I must go. Sorry. There is nothing to make me change my mind, even if it takes more than two years. You just have to understand and be patient until I come back."

"But, Son," his father says, "You told me when you asked for my permission to enter university that you would spend four years there, and then you would be finished. Now you want to go to a foreign country for all this time; are you not thinking of your mother?"

"Don't you ever say that again," the mother says to her husband in an angry manner. "I am going to give him my permission and my blessing to go and to succeed. After all, it is for a better future."

"You are going to give him your permission and your blessing?" the father asks incredulously,

"Yes, and you should too."

George sees that the others outnumber him, he also sees the eagerness in his son's face, and he knows that he cannot stop his son, just like he cannot stop the water from the river for his own field.

"When are you leaving for Canada then?" he asks, and he hopes to hear a good answer.

"In about two months, when my papers are ready."

"Then can you help me plant my summer work before you go?"

Demetre cannot help but laugh at those words.

"Is that why you are so worried, brother? You need someone to help your fields? When do you need to do this?"

"In a few days, maybe next week, depending if I can find the seed and the weather?"

Demetre tells him that they need to return to Athens in a few days since Petros has to start his Canadian Embassy applications, medical exams, and all other the necessary tasks for going abroad.

"Well, at any rate," says George, "if we get a chance, we will do the planting."

They sit back and enjoy the peaceful moments of family life for a while. Then, Petros says to his father, "Father, Uncle and I are thinking of going hunting tomorrow. Is there anything around here we may find?"

"You are going hunting without a permit?" George asks.

"That is right; we'll arrange it. Do you have the guns?" Demetre insists.

"Yes, you can have mine, and my son has his, which his mother has kept hidden for a long time."

Petros is surprised.

"You know your mother; she wouldn't let me touch her son's stuff."

Despina by now has already set the table with her best linen. She serves the food in her best dishes. They all eat with a good appetite and drink to Petros' success. After a few glasses of wine, his father begins to speak more freely, and they have a very pleasant evening.

4

Next day at dawn, Petros and his uncle get up and prepare to go hunting. His mother was up much earlier and hung both guns in the same familiar place with the cartridges beside them. They dress in his father's old clothes, untie the dog, and start out.

"Be careful, Demetre, take care of both of you," Despina shouts at her brother-in-law on their way out.

"Don't worry," they both yell back, then Petros says to his uncle, "We'll go down by the Crystal Spring, where we should be able to come across some thrushes and blackbirds, or even a couple of wild pigeons, and from there, we can go to the marshlands and see whether we can spot a few ducks."

"What about rabbits, nothing this time of the year?"

"Unlikely, yet not impossible; but, we do have the best hound of the area, as my father calls him."

They follow the path through the brambles and the wild plants in the direction to the Crystal Spring. When far enough from the village, they load their guns and walk separately about thirty yards apart. Petros watches his steps carefully, ready to shoot at anything that moves. His uncle, a bit farther down, steps among the branches in the same manner, and the dog stays ahead of both of them, wagging his tail and sniffing around. All attention is on the way the dog behaves, as this is the first indication of wild game being in the area.

Suddenly four thrushes fly up from the bushes. His uncle moves quickly and shoots, and Petros does the same. Each of them kills one bird.

Demetre is excited: "Good stuff. We got two on the first shot."

"I see that you are very good at shooting, Uncle," Petros says to Demetre as he walks over to retrieve the two birds before the dog has his teeth on them. He places both in his bag and smiles with satisfaction.

They continue on their way for a while without spotting anything else and finally reach the Crystal Spring. There, they sit down in the shade of the wild pear trees and rest for a while. Petros goes to the spring to drink some water. The spring is a rectangular reservoir made out of cement, about five to six meters long, two meters deep, and two meters wide. In the front, there is an opening to let the water through a funnel made of cane. The water is cold and refreshing. Petros leans down and drinks some then returns to where his uncle is and sits next to him. The dog lay at their feet with his eyes closed as though he is asleep. His uncle examines the birds closely.

"They are not as fat."

"Yes, this time of year thrushes are not usually fat for the tough time of the cold season they have gone through."

Petros glances around, looking as far as he can see. In front of his eyes are rocks and rugged hills covered in brambles, wild pear, fig, and almond trees. A few maple trees also surround the spring.

"Rugged country, eh?"

"Yes very rugged, although you cannot imagine how it was not too long ago when I was a young man. At least now the villagers have this spring for their fresh water. Not too many years ago people had to get their water from the wells because these dry mountains offered nothing other than being good pastures for the flocks of goats and sheep."

"But, Uncle, these mountains can be transformed into arable land as other people do in other parts of the world. These days with all the machinery at our disposal, the mountains can be terraced in levels, like plateaus, as the experts call them, and of course they can be used after that to grow all kinds of things, like these fruit trees. We are sitting right now underneath a wild pear tree. With proper treatment, they can easily become domesticated. Besides, figs and the almonds also do well here. After the ground is shaped the way it is supposed to, even grape vines and olive trees can grow here because the climate allows them to thrive. It only takes the proper decision to be made. But of course the politicos do not see things the way people do these days, and the junta doesn't care about what people think anyway."

His uncle gets a bit nervous at the sound of these words and looks around to make sure no one is overhearing them.

"You shouldn't be talking this way if you really want to get the chance to go away and study. You know very well what they do when one states things like this out aloud and get heard by others."

Petros is surprised to see him react this way, but he is not at all inclined to stop at this.

"The first step must be taken by the system to provide the agricultural council with the required machinery and proper plans. If something started today, in less than five years the trees would produce big profit. Unfortunately, Uncle, the economic advisors to our government usually do not look this far ahead."

"You are right, but we better go now."

"Yes, let's go. We'll take the other road over the small marsh, and hopefully we can come across some ducks. Then we can go by my father's greenhouse and see what he has accomplished. Sounds okay?"

"Yes, let's get going then."

They follow the road to the marsh. There are a few clouds on the north horizon. No wind, but the weather can change very quickly. A fierce storm could come from the north which can drench everything in a matter of minutes.

"We'd better be quick, Uncle. I don't like the looks of these clouds."

"I don't think this weather is going to change any time soon, Son. Why you are so concerned?"

But his nephew repeats,

"We have to be quick, my uncle. I don't like these clouds."

As they enter the olive grove, Petros catches sight of a wild dove at the top of a tree. He aims and shoots, quickly and with confidence: he succeeds. He reloads and runs to pick up the bird, which is fluttering its wings and half dead on the ground. The dog reaches the bird first. He approached the bird to pick it up with his mouth, but when he comes close to it, the bird flutters and scares the dog away, barking and wagging his tail.

Petros bends down and reaches for the fluttering bird; he can see the huge pain in its eyes. Suddenly, the strange shudder overtakes his body again, like when he was aboard the ship. "What is it?" he asks himself and doesn't feel like hunting anymore.

A light wind starts up just then, and Petros convinces Demetre that they should head to his father's greenhouse. As they set off for their destination, raindrops begin to come down, one by one at first, big raindrops, and full of soil. They increase their pace now, almost running, but they are still soaking wet when they reach the greenhouse.

George welcomes them heartily and teasingly, "Well, well, let me welcome the hunters. How was it?"

"We found a couple things," Demetre says.

"Whatever you caught, it was not worthy of the trouble and the soaking that you went through."

Demetre looks around. "Is this your greenhouse, Brother?"

"Yes, my brother, and I plan to fill it with summer vegetables, like tomatoes and cucumbers and in the fall I'll grow the best winter stuff you can find in the western Crete." Then he turns to his son and asks, "Wouldn't be better, Son, if you get married to this girl Magda who is interested in you, and forget about this trip to Canada?"

Petros turns to Demetre, annoyed.

"Why shouldn't I tell, my boy? They are your parents; they deserve to know everything, don't you think?" Demetre says with a guilty look.

"Brother, you did right by telling us," George says to his brother. "Son, it would be better if you tell us what you intend to do about this."

"I don't intend to do anything right now, Father. I repeat: I don't want to hear about women and marriage before I go away. End of story. Be patient, please. When I want to, we'll talk about marriage."

His answer is sharp and forceful. The brothers decide not to pressure him further.

The rain is heavy, and as it falls on the plastic cover of the greenhouse, it makes a strangely beautiful, even melodious sound. But the storm is as quick as it is strong. After the rain stops, the three of them take the road leading to the village. It is almost noon. A rainbow appears with its many brilliant colors, which gives them a feeling of hope and beauty.

After lunch, Petros and his uncle go down to the café for a cup of coffee. The small place is almost filled, and the air is heavy with cigarette smoke, and fumes from the charcoal-filled brazier in the middle of the room; it is hard on the eyes. Some of patrons are playing cards, two arguing over the backgammon game, and others simply sit around the heater to stay warm. An old man recognizes Demetre and invites him and Petros to come over and sit close to him.

"That man is Gerry, your other uncle," Demetre says to Petros.

"I know, Uncle."

The others make room for them to sit close to the brazier. The mayor is sitting at a table farther across the room; he welcomes them with a nod of his head.

Gerry yells to the proprietor, "Foti, come offer us a drink."

"Alright, alright, Gerry, what do you like to have?"

"Two coffees for our visitors, Foti, and don't pretend you don't know us."

The proprietor laughs at the old man's comment and goes away. Gerry, who is Despina's brother, takes Petros' hand, "Come now look at what I found for you. When I heard you were here I went to the forest and gathered some mushrooms. We'll cook them on the brazier. As I remember, you are quite fond of these, aren't you?"

Petros is quite happy that his old uncle remembers he likes this particular kind of truffle-like mushrooms. When cooked on the charcoal, they taste delicious. He smiles at the old man: "Yes, you know me well, Uncle. Thank you."

Petros' mind flies back to the world of his imagination, a world exactly like this one, simple, pure, hospitable, without a trace of vanity. His blood flows in tune with the blood of those locals, the beats of his heart are in harmony with the lion-like heart of this island, and his soul lies back and rests.

"After you have your coffee, I'll cook them, and the whole shop will be filled with the smell. Let's have a brandy to warm up first."

Demetre turns to ask Gerry, "How did you do with your gardens and melon fields last year?"

"It's always the same, Demetre. Don't you know about these things? Struggles, hardship, and nothing to show for—just like the year before..."

"The big greengrocer companies buy everything," a man sitting next to them says. "This is why we suffer every year. We sweat in the fields from morning to night and have nothing to show for."

Petros listens to the man's comment and then says, "Is there something you can do to correct the situation?"

"Who is going to correct it, my boy? It is a situation that cannot be corrected. Last year, as I recall, we sold our tomatoes for twenty cents per kilo, tomatoes you city people pay two to two-and-a-half dollars per kilo. Where does the rest of the money go? To the pockets of the greengrocers and the middle men! This is not the only problem we have. They also cheat when they weigh our produce. One time, a middleman threw away a few cases of my tomatoes because he said that they were rotten. Total crap! How could my tomatoes get rotten from my field to his warehouse in a day? But who is going to check things for us when we are in the fields all day, and he sends back to us whatever he likes? That's the situation, Petros. Now tell me how can it be corrected?"

Petros says, "From the twenty cents here to the two-and-a-half dollars in the city, there must be something you can do. Why don't you guys team up, all together, and form a co-op? Run it, govern it yourselves and that way, you have a better bargaining power when you deal with the big greengrocers. That way, you demand what you think is fair and leave it up to the middleman to decide whether to pay it or not. Once you control the supply, you can control the price to a certain point."

Everybody in the coffee shop gathers around him, even the mayor. Demetre kicks his nephew's foot to quiet him. He knows some people do not like to hear about change. With the current political situation, even the slightest change can trigger a nation-wide negative reaction from the politicos. However, the young Spathis doesn't want to lower the tone of his voice now that he has their attention. He wants to teach these people some ideas which may inspire them to fight against the system.

"Hey, Yanni, your father is looking for you," someone yells from the open door interrupting the whole conversation.

"Foti, get us another round of brandies," Gerry yells at the proprietor who nods his head.

Petros carries on, explaining to them what they can do: find a good lawyer, write up a mandate for the co-op, elect a governing body, and do whatever it takes to start looking after themselves and not just rely on the existing system to help them.

The villager sitting next to Petros is still not convinced: "You think that an association like that is going to do a better job for us?"

"Yes, definitely. Listen to this: when I go to Athens, I'll find you a good lawyer, then I'll make sure before I go away he gets in touch with you guys, and you take it from there."

Demetre gives him the signal to stop as he is worried what the mayor is thinking about all this. Petros does not listen to his uncle and continues to tell the villagers how to form the co-op and what their rights are. "But what you are telling us to do, Petros, is nothing more than a communist idea, isn't it?" the mayor buts in.

Petros Spathis smiles at him and says, "What I'm saying to you has nothing to do with communism or anything like that. It only has to do with how you can get ahead of the system, which has not helped you so far: nothing more, nothing less."

Petros speaks with passion; he feels deeply for these simple people whom God has blessed by shielding them from the squalor and the misfortune of the city life, but at the same time has cursed by forcing them to breathe their last breath in the fields. He is one of them, he has come from them, and he is proud of it.

His Uncle Gerry says to him, "Let us stop these things now. Is it true that you are going to Canada to study?"

"Yes, Uncle, in about two months."

"How fortunate are you to have the chance to see other people and how they live!"

Gerry is peeling the mushrooms now, and placing them on top of the brazier. Petros orders another round of brandy for everyone and asks his Uncle Gerry,

"Come on now, are you going to tell us one of your stories?"

Gerry looks at him with a warm smile. "What kind of a story?"

"Whatever you want. Tell us a story from the days you were young."

The café fills with the aroma of roasting mushrooms, and someone yells from the back, "Oh, no Gerry, for God's sake, are you cooking your mushrooms again?"

"What are you complaining about? Come closer and get your share. These are the best mushrooms in western Crete." He then turns to Petros, "Well, let me tell you about the time I had this old single-barrel shotgun. I went out one morning with my Habibo, my dog, and climbed up to the top of the mountain in the west, hoping that on our way down the other side we can come across a rabbit, or perhaps a thrush or two. I didn't have a good gun, but I had a good dog, and the dog is more important sometimes."

"Gerry, may the devil take you, are we going to hear the same story again?" Someone shouts from the other end of the coffee shop.

Gerry pays no attention to the man. He takes two mushrooms from the brazier, gives one each to Petros and Demetre, and they clink their glasses.

"Viva! And here is to life! A curse on death!" he says and they all drink the brandy in one gulp.

"As I was saying, the dog picks up a smell, and I follow him. I see him stopping in front of this small bush and wagging his tail and growling. He must have picked up on a rabbit trail, so I go near and see this rabbit inside the bush, in his den not more than five yards away. I aim, but then a thought comes to me: why don't I aim at the tip of his head so I don't ruin the head, which is the tastier part of the rabbit? So I take aim again, but the rabbit jumps out of his den and races for the grape grove. The dog runs after him but the rabbit can run a lot faster than a dog in a grape grove, I will have you know. That's how I lost a rabbit from five yards in front of me. I got so upset that I aimed at a pear tree and unloaded my gun at it."

His eyes are dark and full of fire from excitement, the heat of the brandy in his guts, and the brazier next to him. His brows are raised expressively, giving his face an animated beauty and sweetness. Petros finds the story very funny, but he controls himself, and Gerry orders another round of brandies.

Foti fills up their glasses one more time; they eat another mushroom each and clink again.

"To the health of the tired bodies," Gerry cheers and the others repeat.

Petros is a bit puzzled about the strange cheer.

"He means to the health of the distressed body which suffers the toiling of the field everyday," Demetre tells him.

They sit there for a long time drinking brandy and eating mushrooms. Gerry continues telling stories and downing one glass after another until they have had enough, according to Gerry, who manages to get them all pissed drunk. Petros cannot have enough of the old man's stories and hangs onto his every word. The flames in the old man's eyes and his mannerisms make him appear so natural, so clear, so pure, and so simple yet so full of passion. His hands are rough and calloused, his sleeves torn, his woolen shirt almost worn through. Yet, Petros Spathis loves him so much.

They leave and go home, staggering from one house wall to another until they make it home and both lie down.

Two or three more days go by in the same manner. Petros visits the monastery a couple more times and studies the handwritten correspondences. He finds again within these pages the soul of his ancestors, and their longing for justice and freedom—it seems as though nothing has changed in the last one hundred or so years. His mind tries to find some short of a solution to the big problems in Greece and he can only see some rays of hope in changing of the junta to a democratically elected government, where the voice of the people can be heard.

A few days later, Demetre and Petros depart for Athens. As they get in the taxi for the trip to the port of Souda, Petros Spathis looks at the village, at the square with the puddles where children play. When the taxi drives farther away, he looks again from afar and suddenly has an unexplainable fear for his people. He is leaving behind a part of his soul, here, in this village where he was born, with all the rocks and ruggedness, the simple people, the brandy and mushrooms, and Uncle Gerry's openhearted warmth. Petros promises himself that some day he'll return to stay longer; to live with them, to be reborn amongst them, just as every living being is reborn. Then again this fear overtakes his heart, and he turns to looks at Demetre who is absorbed in his own thoughts.

5

Everything around Petros Spathis always reminds him of time, of the time he needs to secure his visa to leave, time which passes so quickly, like the beats of his heart, like the well-wound clocks in the plazas and the big buildings he visits. The winter passing, the spring passing, the sun now appearing with more and more warmth, the trees, the plants blooming, the birds, the animals reproducing, the people always rushing to keep up with the pace of life, the cars, the ships, the airplanes traveling—all of them stand within the well-designed wall of time.

Three weeks have gone by since they returned from Crete, and with the help of his uncle, Petros finds a good lawyer and forwards the co-op case to him. Any day now he expects to hear news from the dean. He has applied at the Canadian embassy for his visa, and he has an appointment for the medical exams in three days. He sees Eleni often, yet in his mind is the promise to his aunt about calling Magda. He finally finds an excuse not to meet with Eleni and calls this other girl. Magda is excited, and they agree to meet later in the evening, perhaps go to the movies or something.

Maria is happy for his call and cannot wait until he will talk to her mother about it. His uncle Demetre is at home busy with some paperwork when Petros comes down from his room on his way out. Aunt Maria is there and gives him a hug.

"Have a good time, my son. Magda is a very good girl."

He says goodbye to both of them. He walks for about half an hour and finds Magda waiting for him at a small coffee bar they had agreed to meet. She is wearing a blue mini skirt and a white blouse;

she is tall and has a very stylish figure. He leans over to kiss her on her cheek.

"Hello, Magda. Sorry I'm late."

"Hi, Petros, not to worry. I believe I came here a bit early. Would you like to sit down for a while?"

He agrees, and when the server comes he orders two cold coffees. They sit back and chat. She is interested in what he is going to do abroad. He gives her all the details and plenty of ideas of what he expects this place Canada will be.

"I admire your courage," she says, "I don't know if I would have the guts to go so far away for so long. It must be quite stressing."

"Well it can be in a way, although I try not to let it sit in my mind that way. I'm actually excited to go because it will give me the chance to look at how other people in the world do things and how they go about their daily stuff."

She admires his straight forward answer and likes his features. Petros is also attracted to her broad smile and finds his appetite for her body is increasingly heightened minute by minute, something he doesn't hide from her when he leans a bit closer and looks deep in her eyes. He sees a little fire in these eyes, something he hasn't ever noticed in Eleni. She smiles and passes her tongue over her lower lip. He turns to look around; there are a few people in the coffee bar, yet not enough to stop him as he leans a bit farther and his lips touch hers.

"What would you like to do in your life, Magda? Now that you have finished the high school, do you think of going higher?"

"Yes, I'd like to get involved in the movie industry. I enjoy the idea of studios and productions and all those things. I have applied to the Pandas School of Art, a private school which specializes in movie making. Perhaps I am to become a film producer someday."

Now is his turn to admire her aspirations although he knows that her family's connections and money always help when it's needed. He doesn't hesitate to give her some encouragement: "Good for you! That is a field I never thought of, yet it is a fascinating and growing industry. You are going to do well in it. Of course it must take quite some effort in studying everything that is related to the industry."

"Yes, my dad says it may take three years or even longer if I don't apply myself as much."

"Do you plan to apply yourself seriously in this, Magda?"

"Yes, Petros," she says, and her mouth sends him a signal of a kiss. "When I like something and I want it badly, I usually put my best effort in it. One can say I don't like failure under any circumstances."

She leans and lets her lips touch his.

Her words are simple and sharp. Petros now knows that this girl may not stop for anything, this girl who keeps on staring at him and wonders when he is going to make his move and really kiss her. Of course, Petros is willing to do exactly that.

The taste of her mouth arouses all his instincts, and he wants to touch this girl all over. However, they hear the clearing of the proprietor's throat and stop. Petros pulls back, and she gives him her best smile, showing a straight line of teeth and a hungry tongue. They stay there for another half an hour, and then she wants to go.

"What would you like to do now? See a movie?"

He looks at his watch; it is eight o'clock. "Where do you like to go?"

She suggests they go to a movie, and he agrees. They walk to the cinema, and Petros offers her his arm. She takes the chance and leans toward him a bit more. Petros loves that. They get in the theater and realize the place is almost full, so they make their way to the balcony where they notice that it is almost empty. They find two seats. He turns to look at her, and she takes the courage and offers him a long and passionate kiss. His hunger for her body becomes evident. She takes his hand and places it between her legs, a move he takes even further by sliding his hand up and touches her pubic hair. That makes her go wild. He does not let go, and the rubbing of his hand inside her makes her move her body left and right with such intensity that she has an orgasm in a matter of seconds. She then finds his erection and plays with him for a minute or two, but he wants a lot more than that.

"You like to go?" she notices and asks.

"Where are we going?"

"I have a place we can go."

He wonders where this place may be, definitely not her parents' house.

"A friend of mine, she is out of town, I have the key. We can go there."

They walk out of the theater and find a cab. She gives the directions to the taxi driver, and in twenty minutes they are in front of a four-storey apartment building. He follows her inside, and they walk to the second floor where she opens the door of one unit and guides him inside. In a couple of minutes they are naked.

She takes him in her mouth and lets him enjoy her technique of oral sex while she tries hard to find her own orgasm with her hands inside her legs rubbing in a frantic way.

He loves to see Magda's every move, making both of their satisfaction her goal at the same time.

She is so much fun to be with that Petros completely forgets that Eleni is supposed to be his girlfriend.

Two hours later they take a shower together and make their way out of her friend's home. A cab comes and takes Magda back to her house. There, Petros kisses her when she says, "You make sure to call me again, okay?"

He nods. He likes the idea of seeing her again.

The next morning his aunt is anxiously waiting for him to get up and tell her all about his date with Magda. Finally, he comes down from his bedroom at nine o'clock. Maria puts his coffee and toast on a tray and serves him at the table, and asks, "What time did you come home last night? I didn't hear you coming in. How was your date? Isn't Magda a good girl?"

"Yes, I know, Auntie, she is a very pretty and nice girl. I like her a lot. I'm going to see her again the next couple of days."

His aunt feels as if she is flying in the clouds as she hears his comments, then immediately calls her friend, Magda's mother, about all the good news.

Petros spends the rest of his day putting together things for the embassy. The next day, he goes to a clinic for his medical exams. A few days later, he is called for an interview with the Canadian embassy officials. He gets lucky when he meets an embassy clerk named Paul Nickolitch, who is excited when finding out where Petros is going because he graduated from the same university faculty. Paul gives Petros some extra help, fast-tracking his papers.

When Petros returns home in the afternoon, he calls Magda and they agree to meet at the same coffee bar later in the evening.

Just as he gets off the phone with Magda, Eleni calls and sounds upset on the phone, so he agrees to see her that afternoon. He leaves the house and walks for a while until he gets to their usual spot where he sees her waiting for him.

"Hey, how are you?" he asks and gives her a hug.

"I don't know. I don't feel well today," she goes, "I haven't seen you for a couple of days. Why?"

"Eleni, I have been busy with getting myself ready to leave the country. Do not complain, please."

She becomes silent. They sit down and have a couple of coffees without any exchange of words.

Then Eleni opens her mouth, "I want us to get engaged, before you go."

She sounds determined.

He is stunned, and he doesn't like the sharpness of her voice. Her eyes slowly fill with tears.

"I am sorry, but I can't do this now. No, I won't do this now. I will not think of a commitment, any commitment, until I come back from Canada."

"You will never come back to me, Petros. Why won't you admit it? You keep giving me excuses."

"I haven't given you any kind of excuses. I just don't want to tie myself down at this stage of my life before I can be happy with what I have achieved. That's all."

"Then perhaps we should just go our different ways."

She doesn't even believe herself saying that.

"Yes, perhaps it is better this way," Petros sighs and gets up.

They leave the small coffee bar where they met so many times for the last two years. Today, they leave in separate directions.

Petros doesn't want to go back home, so he finds a pool hall where he spends an hour or so until the time comes for him to go and meet Magda.

A bus takes him to the small bar. She is not there yet, so he orders a frappe and grabs a newspaper from the table next to him.

Magda shows up with a huge smile on her face.

Petros looks at her and thinks he is already in love with this happy, bubbly, full-of-laughter and optimism girl. The flame of desire is still alive and thriving in her eyes, and he is very happy to see that. She falls in his arms. They kiss, and everyone in the bar looks at them and smiles.

"Hey, you look so pretty," he says, his eyes traveling all over her body.

She gives him her best smile again.

He orders a coffee for her, and they sit for an hour to chat about this and that. She tells him that her parents have been in the mining business for years. It is a family business; three generations of them have been involved in this line of work. She has a brother, Stefanos, two years older than her, who is being groomed to take control of all the family business in a few years when her father, George Avgeriou, retires. He listens to her, and his eyes are always caught on her two beautiful lips. She sends him a kiss here and there while she talks, a move he loves to see.

She then decides it is time for them to go. He asks whether they can go back to her friend's apartment, but she says her friend is back in Athens, and the place is not available for them today. They stroll to Strefi's Park, a small piece of green in the heart of the city. They walk and talk until they find a bench where they sit. It is a warm May night, and some stars are visible above them. She is wearing a jacket, and he unbuttons it and puts his hand on her breasts. She turns to his side a bit, and they exchange a passionate kiss. The warmth of their bodies turns to an intense sexual hunger that they want to explore to the fullest, yet the park bench is not the best place to do that. They both look around to see if anybody is around. Seeing that they are alone, she takes the courage and goes down on him, which gives him the pleasure he somehow has anticipated all along. He wants to give her some satisfaction as well, but when he tries to touch her, she pushes his hand away and methodically caresses herself. Again, she controls his sexual satisfaction and hers at the same time. Petros doesn't mind that at all. The sounds of the night on the park interplay with their moaning, and as the stars stare at them, their sexual hunger turns to a pleasant consummation.

They take the slow walk toward the lights of the city streets and slowly come to a small plaza where they get a cab. She gives him her mailing address and asks him to make sure he writes to her when he goes to Canada. Her eyes are teary as she says that, and Petros feels a lump in his throat. He may care for this young woman a bit more than what he would like to admit to himself.

Another week goes by, and he gets news from the dean that the University of British Columbia, in Vancouver, Canada, has accepted him as a graduate student in their Masters of Business Administration program for the semester commencing in September, which means he'd better have his papers in order soon. Once he is in Vancouver, he has to find a place to live before school starts and he has to acquaint himself with the city, the bus routes, and all that. The university, UBC, mailed all the necessary papers to his uncle's house, and he realizes that there are even many more forms for him to fill out: registration, selection of courses, et cetera.

Two weeks later, after having everything in order, he gets a call for an interview at the Canadian embassy. He manages to do well at the interview, without any assistance from the translator in attendance. After all, he speaks good English and that, of course, is a plus in helping him get his visa. He arranges for his parents to come to Athens and see him off. The night before his departure he goes out with Magda. She hugs him passionately.

"Petros Spathis, I think I am in love with you. I look forward to hearing from you while you are away, and seeing you when you come back. I may even convince my parents to let me come and visit you at some time. Do you want me to visit you in Vancouver, Petros? Perhaps next summer?"

He smiled at her and kisses her lips.

"You can visit me in Canada anytime, Magdalene. I think I am in love with you as well. I feel sad that we will part. I promise to be in touch."

They part, and he goes home to get all his stuff ready. When walking in, he sees his mother and father sitting with his uncle and aunt, waiting for him. They are excited to see him, and he hugs them and says hi. Then he leaves them there to go upstairs to pack. He puts a few things inside his suitcase and frequently stops to look around, as through seeing for the first time the room he has lived in for the last four and a half years. Up until now he's been so busy taking care of all the details of going to Canada; it is only at this moment that he really feels that he is ready to leave, that tomorrow is his last day in this country. He will leave his country, his parents, relatives, and friends for two years, and most painful of all, he will leave behind Magdalene, whom he admits that he loves very much. Yet his heart is filled with curiosity for the unknown, and he is, to a certain degree, impatient to go, finish his degree, and return home. How many beautiful things are there waiting for him when he returns? First and foremost, it will be to start the position he has been offered.

He buttons a shirt, folds it, and places it in the suitcase. He is going to go without getting emotional; he has prepared himself for this, for his mother's sake, who, he knows, is the weakest of all. He is not much concerned with his dad's reaction. George is hard like granite; he is a person who cannot become emotional, a person who cannot break down over a situation like this one.

A line goes through his mind, "May you always reach higher, may you always see farther . . ." A prominent person in his high school once wished to him, a sentence which still rings in his ears like a blessing, like the harmonious sound of church bell. His aunt repeated those words when he returned from his graduation ceremony, and added "Never forget that you are a Spathis, and you owe it to yourself to succeed."

Petros understands the meaning of those words even more now, the love and trust his family has for him cannot be paid back in any other way but with his success.

"Patience, people who love me and rely on me, patience. Someday you will all be very proud of what you have done, I promise you that," He speaks in his heart.

Finally his case is full. He lifts it up high, so that he can judge its weight. It should be okay. He leaves his room and goes down into the living room. All four are there, waiting to spend their last night with him. He sees their sadness in their forced smiles, an emotion they fight to conceal.

His mother calls him, "Come now sit with us, my son. Just think, tomorrow by this time you will be on your way. You will be getting closer to your destination, and we will still be here, as we are now, only you will be missing."

"Yes, Mother, but I'm only going away for a while; do not forget that."

Maria smiles and adds, "Of course, my boy, you will return. But remember, you must write home frequently, so we can find out how your studies are going."

"You guys think as if I am going to forget completely where I come from. Don't worry yourselves with that."

His father cuts in, "Son, you are an adult, but I want you to be very careful. You are going to a foreign country, your mother and father, uncle and auntie, or friends will not be there. There are only a lot of dangers and troubles. Have your eyes and ears open all the time. You are responsible for yourself."

The old man's voice becomes coarse. Petros looks at his dad and is surprised: tears flow freely down the old man's cheeks. Yet this time, George Spathis doesn't even care to hide his feelings from the rest of the family. Petros goes to his father and gives him a big hug.

"Do not worry. I know where I'm going, and I know what I'm there for. My only concern is to get my schooling done and come back home to find you all. Do not worry. Nothing will distract me from my goal."

"What about Magda, my boy?" his aunt asks.

"Magdalene and I are going to be in touch, and I hope to see her when I come back. She tells me she may even come and visit me in Vancouver next summer. I look forward to that, really. I like this girl a lot."

His mother and father hear these words and feel a bit relieved, although they would prefer if he didn't go away at all.

George gets up to go to the bathroom, and Petros can hear the old man blowing his nose.

Petros goes to the bar and pours a drink for himself. He asks if anybody would like to have one, but they all decline. He walks to the window and stares outside: under the dim lights, trees are spreading their shadows silently on the street; cars go by from time to time to mysterious places.

They get up early in the morning even though his flight does not leave until the afternoon. Sadness is all over the whole house. All five know that later in the day, one of them will be absent from the family dinner.

At eleven o'clock Demetre calls a taxi, and in a few minutes the driver honks the horn outside the house.

All five members of the Spathis family get into the cab. They ride to the airport together, looking at the traffic and the scenery of the big city without saying anything. In the airport, chaos greets them: people going in every direction, friends and relatives seeing their loved ones off, clerks and workers milling around, incoming and outgoing flights being announced over the speakers.

Petros takes his suitcase to the check-in counter to be weighed. The airline official gives him his boarding pass; he is supposed to be in the plane in three quarters of an hour. He stops by the currency exchange kiosk to get some extra Canadian dollars, his family following him wherever he goes, noticing every move he makes. After he collects his money, they go to the lounge to sit for a while before he must go through the international flights gate where they cannot follow him anymore.

"Just two years, and I'll be back. Right here we'll meet and I'll have my MBA on hand," Petros tries to give them some thread of hope to hold onto while he's gone.

His mother starts crying, not able to help herself. The emotions overwhelm her, and a trip such as this one scares her so much that she just cannot cope with it, at least not at this time. He hugs his mother, and his eyes start to get teary too. He'd better get through this now before it gets even worse. He takes his mother by the arm, and they walk toward the gate. He hugs and says goodbye to everyone, and then he hugs his mother again and kisses her.

"Goodbye to you; I'll see you in two years."

"Goodbye, my boy," his uncle and aunt say.

"Goodbye, Son," his father says, and his mother adds: "With our blessings. Take care of yourself . . ."

His father searches his pocket and brings out a rosary: he wants Petros to have it and remember him by it. As he gives it to his son, his eyes fill with more tears. The granite has broken down. Petros has never seen his father in tears before last night. He hugs the old man with force and says goodbye to his dear aunt and uncle for last time before going through the gate.

Once in the international departure area, he buys a magazine from the newsstand and sits down to read to keep his mind occupied until the airline officials announce his flight. A short while later his flight number is called over the speaker. He follows the stewardess along with the rest of the passengers to the aircraft. He finds his seat; his mind is still on the ground, with four people he just left behind.

The flight attendants finish their safety demonstration, and in a few minutes the plane soars to the sky. It is so superb to look at the world from such a height!

His trip is uneventful as they fly over Europe to Amsterdam, where they land for refueling and must stay inside the aircraft. Then the plane is in the air again, and the longer part of the trip commences over the Atlantic Ocean, to Montreal. They come across some turbulence over the ocean; however, they get to Montreal without any problem. All passengers disembark because they have to take a different plane for the remaining part of the trip to Vancouver. Since this is the first time he steps onto the Canadian soil, Petros also has to go through Canadian customs. As he waits in line to show his passport and visa to an official, an old woman asks him in Greek, "Hello, young man, can you please help me with my papers?"

The woman reminds him of his mother back home. He smiles at her and asks, "How can I help you?"

"I don't speak a word of English. Please help me when I get to the man behind the counter . . ."

"Oh, sure. Don't worry. I'll help you." He is glad that at least he can converse in English.

When they approach a friendly immigration officer, he translates for her, and she is grateful.

They spend an hour in the Montreal airport. Then they board a different plane, and soon they take off for Vancouver, at the other end of the country. Petros Spathis could never have imagined that it takes almost the same time they spent flying over the Atlantic to reach Vancouver. This is his first understanding of the size of this large country. On this part of his trip he sits next to a young Canadian man who is quite talkative. His name is Tom, and he tells Petros that he works in the logging camps and that he has his folks in Vancouver whom he is going to visit. He asks Petros what is his reason of such a long trip. When Petros says that he is going to attend school at UBC, Tom is surprised.

"Why, you're coming all the way out here for school? Aren't there these kinds of schools back in Greece?"

Petros explains to him that the MBA program they offer in Canada is not available in Europe, and Tom grins at that.

Tom then asks Petros to let him see some Greek drachmas. He says he has been in a few countries around the world and has a collection of foreign currencies. Petros takes a fifty-drachma bill from his wallet and gives to him. Tom looks at it and smiles, "Hey, it looks strange. How many dollars is this worth?"

"Just over a dollar and a half, you can keep it if you like, for your collection."

Tom is elated and puts his newfound treasure in his wallet. When the air attendant comes by, Tom orders two drinks which they both enjoy on their way to Vancouver. The rest of the flight goes by quickly and the pilot tells them that they are just about to land at their destination and they should to fasten their seat belts.

Petros looks down from the window. It is a cloudless night. He has a superb panoramic view on the city, full of lights flickering in the dark. He can distinguish the streets and the tall buildings as the aircraft slowly descends.

They land, and Petros gets up to take his carry-on bag from the overhead compartment, steps off the plane, and says goodbye to Tom. An airline official leads Petros down the long hallways to the baggage area. He finds his suitcase from the appropriate carousel and makes his way to the arrivals area where people wait for their friends and family members. Happy voices are everywhere; people embrace one another, kissing, laughing, and crying. He turns around as if to see someone he knows. There is no one here, he knows, and this is his first bitter moment of realization that he is so far away from people he loves. He wishes Magda was here, but soon he asks himself, "And now, where are you going, Petros?"

He goes and sits on a couch. His eyes catch the old woman whom he helped in Montreal; she sees him too. At the same time, a very tall man with a good-looking woman approaches the old woman who hugs the man and stays in his embrace for quite a while. Petros realizes the man is probably her son. Then he sees her pointing out Petros to the tall man, who starts walking toward him.

"Are you new in the city?" The man asks in Greek.

"Yes."

"I'm going through downtown Vancouver. Do you have anybody to come and meet you here?"

"No, I want to find a hotel to stay."

"Okay then, come along, I'll give you a ride to a hotel that I know," the man says, introducing himself as Jimmy.

"I am Petros Spathis." he shakes hands with Jimmy and smiles, realizing that his problem of where to go is suddenly solved, for now.

They drive through Vancouver. By now it is completely dark. In about half an hour they stop in front of a hotel with the name "Ambassador," and Jimmy gets out and goes inside to speak with the front desk person. He comes back in a few minutes and says to Petros, "Come along, I found you a room." He takes Petros in the hotel and pre-pays his bill for one night and then gives him a note.

"This is my home phone number. Take this and go upstairs and rest. If you need something, don't hesitate to call me, okay?"

Petros cannot thank him enough. The clerk passes him his keys and he goes upstairs to his room. So this is his first night in Vancouver. Thoughts fill his mind, strange thoughts in a strange place. Where is he? Who is he? Why is he here? What does he want?

Soon drowsiness overcomes him, and he goes to sleep.

The next morning he wakes up late: ten-thirty. He opens his window, and the sun fills his room. Hope and optimism return to him.

He walks out of the hotel and wonders around the city. The clean fresh morning air makes him feel reborn. He enters a café to get a cup of coffee. Sitting down, he slowly sips his beverage, observes the people going in and out and the waiter busy taking orders from the customers. After finishing his coffee and not knowing what else to do, he decides to go out and find the proper bus to the university he is about to attend in about three weeks. He better go and see what it takes for the registration and that. Someone helps him find his bus stop. He boards the bus and notices there is nobody to collect the fare; instead there is this box where the driver tells him he has to put the money. He realizes he doesn't have any change for the fare other than a twenty-dollar bill. The driver is very understanding and takes a quarter from his own pocket to put in the box for Petros. Amazed, he thanks the driver and sits close by, expecting him to tell him where to disembark.

The ride lasts for about twenty minutes. He likes the surroundings very much. The weather is good, and he is able to see clearly for a good distance. Green grass is everywhere, and the houses along the road each has its own property, with lawns, gardens, passageways, and pavilions for the cars. They are built in a medieval style, like mansions in the most exclusive neighborhood back home. The streets are wide and nicely landscaped with trees on both sides. It is a world so different from the one he knows up to now: much more beautiful, elegant, and filled with green.

UBC grounds cover a large area. There are many buildings, lecture halls, laboratories, swimming pools, student residences, huge parking lots, and a stadium covering a huge area. He cannot believe what is unrolling before him. He has never seen such a beautiful place anywhere before in his life. He spends a long time walking around the campus until he finds himself on a small hill. A student passing by is able to tell him where he has to go to register for his program. He follows a hallway and arrives at the registration office. When his turn comes, he hands his papers to the clerk, who reads them carefully and sends him to the director's office next door. Petros enters hesitantly, but then the director welcomes him with a warm handshake. Petros tells the friendly director who he is and where he comes from and what are his objectives at this university. The director counsels him on the required procedures and tells him that his paperwork is in order; all he needs to do is to meet with an advisor to select the proper courses needed for his MBA program.

When finishing his meeting with the director, he goes out. The sun is still prominent on the horizon. He decides to walk back to the city by following the bus route, whistling and quietly singing. He admires the area, the houses, the streets, the sky. He imagines that he is on another planet, and that quite suddenly something completely strange may happen. But he soon realizes that this is not another planet; it is the same Earth that he lives and moves on. It is just that people here live in a more beautiful place, totally different from his home back in Athens.

After a while he manages to reach the center of the city and goes to eat at the same café he had his coffee earlier.

In the afternoon, he starts looking for a room to rent. After numerous disappointments, he finally succeeds in finding one, and in the very same evening he is able to sleep in his new home. It is a small room with a table, a chair, a closet for his clothes, and a single bed. The size of the room is no more than two by three meters, with paint cracks all over; some paint is peeled right off the walls. He doesn't really care about its condition. It is a very cheap room. A small window with shutters opens to the street, and sees there is a small garden. He takes out his clothes from the suitcase and hangs them with care in the closet. Then he sits down on the bed and decides to write home and let them know he has arrived and is okay, three letters to three different addresses.

Realizing he has no paper, he goes out to the closest corner store where he buys some paper and goes back to his room to write. He describes in detail that his trip was very good, that the city is beautiful, and that he feels very enthusiastic about the university. He writes with intense feelings, particularly in the letter addressing Magdalene. He signs the letters and seals the envelopes. He will post them first thing tomorrow morning. His thoughts go back to whom he left behind, and his heart tightens. He picks up a book to read, so that he can escape from the torment for a moment. He turns the pages, yet in every page he sees a familiar beloved face, or two blue eyes—his mother's, filled with tears, looking at him sadly. He wonders how she is doing without him. A strange shudder overtakes his body, and a fear goes through his spine.

Slowly his eyelids become heavy, and he falls asleep.

6

The impressions of the first days fade away slowly with time and Petros Spathis gets closer and closer to his goal. He follows his studies with zeal, without wasting any time. His uncle sends him money regularly, and the funds from the scholarship arrive on time every month. This income takes care of his expenses, leaving him free of money worries to concentrate on his work. This is also why he is able to move to the university's dorm, a much more spacious place which he shares with a roommate. He reads endlessly, he learns, he attends lectures and seminars; he studies and writes all the required exams that are scheduled from time to time. He notices his grades are excellent, and the way the professors and the TAs treat him is phenomenal. Sometimes his creativity leaves them all completely astonished because he is also very good with practical things. His perspicacity and thoughtfulness even have his professors in wonder. The solutions he suggests for many problems are straight forward, based on solid ground, and at the same time doable. Many a time he challenges a professor or TA with his analysis.

He gets to know many other students, making friends with a few that he chooses with care. They visit his dorm room at times, or he goes to theirs to talk, to discuss school subjects, or to spend pleasant evenings socializing. Except for the mornings when he attends classes, the rest of the day he spends studying, and his leisure activities only occupy a couple of hours of his day. He meets a couple of girls, one of whom he is really fond of. Her name is Samantha, and she comes from an Italian family. Her dad owns a restaurant in Vancouver. Sometimes Petros goes with Sam to the place to enjoy a lunch or dinner.

He stays informed of the current affairs in Greece and with the junta government, and is quite surprised to meet a few Greeks in Vancouver who even support and approve of the military government that dictates all the rules back home. He argues with them, but not vehemently. More often, he gets involved with the city's most prominent Greek association in Vancouver called the Greek Community of Vancouver, located on Arbutus Street, which has a Greek-language elementary school, a Greek Orthodox Church, and a community center.

He keeps in touch with his relatives by writing to them often, and he also sends them a picture or two once in a while, just to make them feel better and let them know they don't have to worry about him; he is really doing okay. Magda writes to him and lets him know she is planning to take a trip to Vancouver sometime the next summer, which is only six months away. His parents send a few letters, but Demetre and Maria write to him more often.

What he enjoys the most is the way of life of the Canadians, their "take it easy" attitude and their simple, pleasant outlook about life in general. He can understand that because he knows Canadians haven't gone through occupation by the Germans in the Second World War, or the dictatorship of a junta. But what he likes about the people the most is that they start a conversation with you at any time, at any place, either on the street, or in the bus. They can talk to you about anything without caring whether it interests you or not. They are mostly polite and cheerful, and they help you if they can. They don't care who you are or what you are wearing, or how you talk, as most Canadians speak with an accent. Petros' accent is so profoundly distinct that one can tell quite easily he is Greek. But it doesn't matter to them at all.

He writes all these things to his relatives and Magda with such enthusiasm that at one time he asks her whether she can see herself living with him in this country. He is surprised to get her positive answer in her letter which comes rather quickly. He likes to hear that she has the blood of the gypsies in her veins; she can go away from her home at any time if the circumstances are the right ones.

He enjoys knowing that because he is also a man who loves to travel, to move around, to visit and discover new places and new people.

A letter from Demetre tells him that his father is a bit tight financially, and it has to solely subsist from the money he invested in the greenhouse. The produce that he hopes to get him on his feet will not be profitable until next summer. Petros decides to look around and see whether he can get a job so he can send some money to his dad. However, he is on a student visa and it is difficult to get work outside the campus. He asks people in the Greek community for help, and Samantha talks to her dad, and soon enough Petros is hired for part-time work in his restaurant as a cleaner in the kitchen.

With this new employment, Petros makes a couple of hundred dollars extra a month, which he can send it back to his parents. This of course gives Samantha the chance to see him more often, which he doesn't mind at all.

His mid term exams come in the month of January. He takes leave from his job for a while in order to concentrate on the task on hand. He writes and studies everyday until late in the night, but his efforts are rewarded when he is awarded the best possible marks. He is now in the process of organizing for the second part of the year, with a couple of weeks of leisure time in between. He returns to the restaurant and meets Ginno, Sam's dad, right at the door.

"Hello, Petros, good to see you. How are you?"

"I'm very good, Ginno. Do you have any work for me? I have a few hours to spare everyday for the next little while."

"Of course I do, Petros. Welcome back. Come and have a coffee. Samantha is here too. I'll give you a schedule."

Petros finds Samantha working behind the bar.

"Hey, how are you?"

"I'm good; the exams are done, I suppose?"

"Yes, I want to get a few hours of work, and your dad says he will fix me up with something. Until the courses start again in a couple of weeks,

I'll be more or less free."

She comes out from behind the bar and hugs him.

"I'm glad to hear that. Perhaps I get the chance to see you a bit more often," she says and kisses his lips.

Ginno walks over from the office in the back and gives him the schedule. He reads it and sees he has five days of four to six hours of work per day. That will get him busy for the next little while.

"Thank you, Ginno. I'll start tomorrow if you want."

"Yeah, tomorrow is good," Ginno says and leaves them alone.

Samantha grabs his arm before he makes a move toward the door.

"Wait for me here for a few minutes. When I'm done, we go together."

Her eyes are burning him; he feels the need to touch her again, so he sits down on a barstool. Fifteen minutes later they both leave for his dorm. They spend the afternoon enjoying the pleasures of their sexuality to the fullest.

Two weeks go by quickly, and Petros Spathis goes back to his full-time studies in business for the second part of the year. His courses are a full load, and he has quite a few reports to prepare. He is always busy with his studies except when he finds the opportunity to meet with Sam and have their "casual thing," as they call their lovemaking. He has top grades in all courses, and he reports all his academic progress to his folks back home.

Despite his busy schedule, Petros also finds chances to intermingle with the other Greek people he has met in Vancouver. Many a time he gets invited to a home for dinner or just a coffee and some socializing activities. He likes associating with these people; in a way, he belongs to them since they all come from under the same sun and talk in the same language, and they all have the same nostalgia for Greece. He enjoys these gatherings a lot: quite a few of these Greeks are well educated. Others may not have university degrees, but are always interested in current events. They live harmoniously and religiously within the community, according to the ideals of their far away homeland.

He also finds the Greek-Canadians well organized. When they need to run the community programs, the schools, the churches, et cetera, they go to their community hall to discuss issues and vote.

He is quite interested in the way the Greek Orthodox Church takes care of matters: most decisions are made by a committee which is also there to defend the rights of the parish, set up functions with the goal of bettering the lives of all in the community. The church offers Sunday services and all the other religious ceremonies. The Sunday school is the place for more extensive Christian and civilized education. He admires their efforts, and sometimes he thinks to himself that if he is to come back here, he will offer whatever he can toward these beautiful ideals. Naturally, small differences and arguments are not absent, but he knows very well: it is impossible for such things not to exist.

He gets closer to the end of the first year, and the exams are the final effort he has to make. After that, all he has to write is his dissertation, which will take at least six to eight months. Magdalene ensures that she will visit him in August. This will give him enough time to finish his exams, get the results, and work for a while at Ginno's to put some money on the side for them to spend when she is here.

There are times when he sits silently imagining that he has finished his schooling, that he has received his diploma, and that he will soon be on his way home. His dream carries him to the happiest moments of seeing his family again at the airport after such a long time. He clings onto the dream as if he depended on it.

During this period, he also finds the time to gather the information requested by the dean from the school back home. He puts together a small report for him and mails it out. The dean writes back to him and expresses his appreciation, and from then on, they keep in regular contact. The dean does not hesitate to mention to him that his job is waiting for him when he comes back and that things are slowly improving back home.

Time never stays still, and his examination time finally comes. Petros does his best to prepare for the battle. He feels like a soldier starting off to war, just like those he sees in films. But he knows he is more prepared than ever, and is very sure of his results. He has tremendous decisiveness and optimism, just as he has shown in all other exams up to now.

The first exam day comes, and he gets up early, bathes, shaves, dresses, and goes to his classroom as early as possible. It is his belief that if the first day of exams goes well, all others to follow will be just as successful. Then the supervisors arrive, and distribute the exams. Petros starts to work with patience. The supervisors walk around; one of them passes by Petros and stands for a while, looking at the work he has finished so far. Then without any comment the supervisor continues on, but not before Petros has distinguished, with his observant eye, a faint smile of satisfaction on the man's face. When done, he hands his paper to the professor at the desk who says, "Thank you, Spathis. Have a good day."

"Good day to you too, Professor," he says and walks outside.

The rest of Petros' exams pass in the same manner. All he has to do now is to wait for the posting of the results. He knows how to judge his work objectively, no different from the way his teachers do, and he is certain that everything has gone well. The same night, he writes back home, letting them know that his first year is over, and there is nothing more for him to do other than write his dissertation, and that will be that.

A few days later, one of the teachers calls him. He tells Petros to meet him at the university. The following morning, his professor greets him with a smile and informs him that the school has approved a bursary for him to help out with his expenses since he has done so well in his exams. He immediately realizes that everything has gone well although the results are not officially posted yet.

"Congratulations, Mr Spathis. I am very happy to give you this good news, and I hope that your excellent progress will continue in the final phase of your studies," the professor says to him pleasantly.

Petros is overjoyed and promises to carry on with the same way as he has done so far. He goes out and feels as though he is up in the clouds. He is now able to send some money home without having to struggle to make ends meet over here.

As he is absorbed in his thoughts, he hears his name called from behind. He turns and sees Samantha.

"Hi, Petros, what brings you to school today? Haven't you finished all your exams?"

He smiles and tells her what happened. She looks at him with admiration.

"I wish I could do as well as you. I'm afraid I failed one course, which means I have to take it again next year."

"Oh, I'm sorry to hear that, Sam. Where are you heading?"

"Well, now that you asked, I'm thinking to take you away for a couple of hours."

He tries to appear hesitant.

"Where do you want to take me, Sam?"

"To my place, you dummy."

She smiles, and he sees her straight line of white teeth.

He leans and kisses her lips, which she finds quite enjoyable.

A couple of days later he goes to school and starts gathering the necessary materials for his dissertation. He finds what he needs and as he heads back to his dorm, he crosses paths with one of his professors who stops him with a smile.

"I see you are getting started with your thesis, Mr Spathis."

"Yes, if I am to finish at some time, I'd better do this now."

"But Mr Spathis, a bit of a break is going to do some good too. Take yourself on a short holiday. I'm sure when you start, it won't take you long to finish."

Petros smiles back, "I will, sir, thank you."

He goes back to his dorm, puts all books on the bed, and sits back to take a deep breath: "This is it. Two semesters and this is the last thing keeping me away from my family and my career. What kind of a break do I need to give myself? Hell, not a long one, definitely."

He sits by his desk, taking paper and pencil to compose the outline the thesis has to follow over the next few months before it becomes presentable to his supervisor.

He ends up sitting in the same spot since mid day, studying. It is now evening. Many a time his eyes leave the lines of the books to look onto the street below his window. The quietness and serenity of the night gives him a strange sensation. The streetlight on the corner illuminates a bright circle on the ground. A man passes with his hands in his pockets, and then he stops underneath the light, looks at his watch, and continues on his way with a faster pace. There is hardly any wind and not even a leaf on the trees moves. Suddenly he feels an inexplicable agony: it is as if something squeezed his heart. He does not know what it means. Maybe someone back home is not well. He puts the books aside to write a letter to his parents. He describes to them what just happened and how he wants to hear them telling him that everyone and everything are okay. He begs them not to hide the truth if anything happened to them. He knows that by morning all this is probably going to be the previous night's false excitement; however, he continues to write, and after finishing it, he seals the letter and promises himself to post it early the next morning.

While he forces himself to go back to his books, he notices a car turning at the corner, and for a moment its lights hit his window and blind him. He stops reading and closes his book. His mind travels and he finds himself fall into a state which he cannot even explain, even to himself. He feels he is away somewhere, flying and looking for something. Stormy waves appear from nowhere, tempestuous and breaking on the rocks. He then realizes he is watching a battle, an eternal war. He sees the battles on the sea and the sieges on the land: well-organized armies, ruthless attacks, but equally cunning defenses.

Everywhere he turns he sees a war taking place, a war just like what everyone has been telling him since the moment he first began to understand the world: two armies, both claim to be right, both propose demands, sometimes one side wins, sometimes the other, and they always leave in their wake the bodies of the innocent, the bodies of people who could have been more useful alive, whose death always results in nothing better.

Is he in a prophetic dream state, or is he imagining all this?

He is now on a strange path up a steep trail. He is alone and barefooted. The stones cut the soles of his feet, which bleed as he continues his climb. His blood is rushing out, making a red flood. He goes on and on alone. On his head he wears a straw hat; the sun is not blinding his eyes, yet it is as if he is blind, following the trail upwards without really seeing anything. How is it that his feet follow this trail to the top of this hill? Why is he wearing this straw hat? He takes it off and throws it away. The wind passes through his long hair, and he goes on, despite wanting to stop. However, an unknown force is pushing him up, and he has to carry on. His blood paints the stones and the gravel of the trail, and the wild thorns pierce his flesh. He continues. At another turn he senses that he is soon at the end of the climb. He finds the courage to go faster, but he is still blind. Suddenly his face gets lit by this phenomenal light emanating from somewhere in front of him. He feels dazzled: is it someone there, or is he alone as always? The strong light is still here in front of his eyes, and a heavenly cry suddenly comes out of his mouth, a scream, a voice he cannot agree is his, yet he hears it as from the depth of his essence.

"*Why? Why?*"

A smile comes in front of his eyes, a smile. Whose smile is this?

Petros Spathis finds himself sitting alone again at his small table looking outside of his window. His neglected book seems to be complaining to him. Yet he doesn't feel like studying anymore. He leans back on his chair, still wondering what just happened. The phone rings, and it is Samantha on the other end.

"Hi Petros. How are you?"

"I'm okay. What's up?"

"I'm close by; you want to hook up?"

"Sure, come along."

Ten minutes later she is in his room. She looks very pretty in her mini-skirt and a dark green blouse. He admires her looks, which she enjoys very much. She hugs him, and their lips lock. A few minutes later they lie naked on his bed where all the books had been earlier.

She climbs on top of him, giving him all she knows to make both of them happy.

A little later, when both of them are satisfied, she says, "You have already started your thesis?"

"Yeah, I have to get it going slowly."

She knows very well why he is in such a hurry; he has told her many times, yet she always hopes that he will change his mind at one point, even if that happens the last day he is here. She gets up, a bit upset.

"I'm going to have a shower."

He follows her to the bathroom, and they hop under the warm stream water. He rubs her gently. Slowly her arousal becomes obvious, so is his. She leans over and takes him in her mouth. He gets truly excited then takes her in his arms and carries her to bed where they make passionate love once again.

Time flies as Petros Spathis keeps busy with his thesis and his work at Ginno's. He sees Samantha quite often, and they have their casual sex. To his surprise, he finds himself quite attracted to her in a different way; his feelings to her have developed over their time spent together. He wonders what to do as he expects Magda to show up in Vancouver by August, and he doesn't like to play both women at the same time. The most frightening thing for him is that they both may want marriage; he doesn't want to tie himself down with anybody at this stage of his life, more so with Samantha, because he knows he has to go back to Greece within the year.

July arrives and he works some long hours at Ginno's. His bank is in good shape, and he keeps sending funds to his parents. He writes to Magda regularly and really looks forward to seeing her. She has given him the detail of her trip and is to fly from Athens to Frankfurt, then to Vancouver and arrive at YVR, Vancouver's international airport, on August the fourth at five o'clock in the afternoon. He goes shopping and buys a couple of shirts and a pair of good pants, something he does for the first time in this country. In the meantime, his dissertation is coming along fine, and he expects to submit it to the faculty in January. Then it will be a matter of two or three months before he receives his degree, and, he can leave Canada for good.

One night while he is at work, Ginno calls him to the side.

"Hey, sit down for a moment, Petros. I have a question for you."

Petros pours himself a cup of coffee and sits next to the boss.

"Well, my boy, you are just about done, I guess. What now?"

"What do you mean, Ginno?"

"Are you going to stay and find a job here, Son, or are you really going back home?"

Petros is caught by surprise because he knows that Ginno knows he is going back to Greece after his studies are complete; why the question... "I'm going back, Ginno, I think you know that. As soon as I have the paper on hand, I am a goner," he says with a laugh.

"I am just thinking, Petros, you know I only have one child and everything I have one day will all be hers. Maybe you'd like to think about it before you decide to really leave the country," Ginno says, looking deep in Petros' eyes.

Petros now knows why. He is glad that Ginno has come out to him like this. He is very sorry, though, to disappoint him.

"Ginno, I really want to thank you for seeing me this way, and I'm very sorry that my mind is made up. But I have to go back. My path lies in Greece. It is a path I have chosen, and I intent to follow, no matter where it leads me. Again, thank you very much for the offer. I would love to stay here and get involved seriously with Samantha, if I could."

Ginno smiles at him and leaves the conversation there.

The days of July quickly go by, and the time finally arrives when Petros is to go and fetch Magda from the airport. He puts on the new clothes and hails a cab to take him to YVR. When he arrives, it is still an hour and a half before she arrives, so he buys a magazine and sits at the waiting hall. He checks the big arrivals/departures monitor and sees that her flight will be on time. He keeps looking at his watch, and finally the monitor says her flight has arrived. He stands where he expects her to show up and waits. His watch now is giving him the hardest time in his life; every minute seems to be eternity. But then, there she is at the end of a long line, exiting the international arrivals gate with a small bag and looking so pretty that Petros Spathis feels that he cannot breathe.

He walks to her, and she smiles and falls in his arms.

"Welcome to Canada, Magda."

"Hello Petros"

They kiss for a long time.

He puts his arm around her shoulders, and they walk outside, where he gets a taxi to his place. Luckily, his roommate is away to Eastern Canada visiting his family, so Petros is alone in the dorm room until the end of August. Therefore, as soon as they arrive, they jump right in bed and start to enjoy each other's body.

"I'm so happy you made it. What magic did you use on your folks?" Petros asks her when they are relaxed.

"I made it clear to my dad I was going and there was no argument. Believe it or not, I got a lot more problems with my mom than my dad."

"I love you, Magda."

"I love you too, Petros."

They don't want to get out until they are both hungry. They get on the bus and go to Ginno's for dinner. There they find not just Ginno, but Samantha as well. Petros introduces Magda to both of them, and they are happy to meet her.

"Now I know why he wants to go back home so fast," Ginno says, looking at Magdalene.

For a while Petros panics because this may be a dangerous situation having both Magda and Samantha together, yet his fears are only his as the two girls are having a good time talking and laughing about girl things. Before Petros takes Magda to go back to Greece, the girls promise to meet again and spend some more time together.

Petros and Magda have now spent ten days together. Their feelings develop even further, and they share a deep love for each other. They both know this happiness is ephemeral since she will go back to Greece tomorrow, and he is to stay behind on his own finishing the last part of his schooling. They enjoyed visiting to various tourist attractions in the city, and Petros never hesitated to take her to everyplace he could. Wherever they could go with a bus, they did. Petros never bothered to get his driver's license in Canada, an affair easier to attend than back in Greece, but he is not in any hurry since his chance of buying a car is so far in the future. He takes Magda to Stanley Park, the Capilano Suspension Bridge in North Vancouver, and they went on a longer trip outside the city to Horseshoe Bay and had lunch there. They even visited the valley around outlying towns Mission and Maple Ridge.

This morning they stay in bed a bit longer to enjoy the pleasures of their sexuality before they have to start worrying about getting ready for her to return to the airport. Her flight is in late afternoon; they should have plenty of time to have lunch at Ginno's, and she can say goodbye to Samantha and her father. Both Petros and Magda feel sad for their parting, yet the idea of him coming back home soon lifts their spirits up, and they hop in the shower together.

Outside it is a very bright and warm day. The sun is very strong, and most people on the streets are in colorful light shirts and shorts. The summer birds are all around, jumping and making their heavenly sounds. The mountains look even prettier than before from Petros' window. Magda sighs when seeing all this. Petros has taken her to the beaches a few times, and she enjoys very much the view with its unique vistas. Vancouver is indeed one of the most beautiful places on earth, and she has made that comment many times to Petros. She even said to him once that she would love to live here if he ever considered the idea of relocating. They both agreed to give it some serious thought in the future.

When they walk into Ginno's Samantha welcomes them and gets them a table. They sit, and Samantha brings a couple of coffees and joins them.

"So the time has come, eh?"

"Yes, it is time for me to go back," Magda says.

"One day I may come and visit you guys in Greece."

Petros and Magda are surprised to hear her saying that, but both soon smile, as Magda says, "Now that is a good idea, eh, Petros? Sam can visit us any time when she is in Greece, can't she?"

"But of course," he says politely.

"You guys have a ride to the airport? If you don't, I'll take you there," Samantha volunteers.

"Oh, thank you, Sam."

They sit back for a while and eat their lunch. Ginno joins them for a few minutes although the restaurant is crowded with customers.

At four o'clock, Samantha gives them a ride to YVR. After parking the car, Sam walks with them into the airport, and Petros asks her, "You are not in a hurry to return to the restaurant, Sam?"

She looks around the airport as if she wants to find someone she knows, and then she turns and tells him, "No, there is no hurry. I'll stay and when Magda goes, I'll give you a ride back home."

They find the airline, and Magda has her baggage checked-in. They then sit at a small bar and have a drink. Time goes by, and when Magda has to go to her gate, they all get up and walk there together. Magda hugs Samantha and says goodbye to her, then she hugs Petros and kisses his lips.

"I love you, Magdalene. Have a good trip and write to me as soon as you get home."

"I promise, I will write. I love you very much and look forward to seeing you home soon." Her eyes get teary.

He holds on to her for a couple of seconds and doesn't want to let her go. She kisses him one last time and walks through the gate.

Samantha quickly takes him by the arm, and they walk to the parking lot and get in her car.

"You love her, don't you?"

"Yes, I love her, Sam."

"I know, and I don't blame you. She is such a pretty and lucky girl."

She starts the car and drives slowly, and he looks outside silently.

When they reach the city and Sam asks, "You want to go home or you want me to take you someplace else?"

He brings his mind back to earth, and turns to her, saying, "Why don't we go to the restaurant? Perhaps your dad has some work for me today, which will keep me busy for a while."

Indeed Ginno has a few hours of work for him, so he spends five hours in the kitchen. He cleans countless dishes, but his mind is on the beautiful face of Magdalene he loves to kiss, and now she is in the clouds traveling back to Greece. Time flies and he finishes all his work around ten thirty. He cleans himself up and is ready to go when Sam comes and takes him to her car.

"Don't worry. I'll give you a ride and then I'll go home."

They get to his dorm room. She wonders whether this is the time for her to have him, or, if it is time for her to go. So she looks at him expectantly, "Anything else I can do for you?"

"Let me have a shower, Sam."

No more words, they both undress and get in the shower. Rubbing each other, they both get so excited that it is just impossible to stop. She takes him in her mouth, and he can't wait to enter her again. He carries her to the couch where they decide to stay and feed the hunger of each other's body.

7

Petros Spathis scrutinizes his face carefully in the mirror to see if he can notice any difference. Maybe these past months that have quickly gone by have left some mark on his skin, but he cannot see anything out of the ordinary. He gets up this April morning with his optimistic attitude in place; he submitted his thesis to the faculty and now he will have his graduation paper in hand today; he cannot hide his excitement.

The winter cold has been slowly driven away by the warm spring air, and the people of Vancouver can be seen wearing lighter coats and hats, and perhaps even just the odd T-shirt is needed to keep warm. At this time of year, it rains in Vancouver more than the people want, but up in northern British Columbia the mountains are still full of snow. Even the tops of the mountains close to Vancouver are still white, and people who love the winter sports still get themselves to the slopes.

He shaves and whistles one of his favored tunes while getting ready to go to the university. He is now certain that in a couple of weeks, he is going back home, to his family. Most importantly, he has gone through the battle, he has fought bravely, and he has the reward to show for it. He feels quite proud of his achievement and knows the time for him to talk is getting nearer and nearer by the day. The last year and a half he has only listened learned, studied, achieved, observed, and decided. Finally the time has come for him to go and put to use all he has learned for the betterment of all the people of his country. The voice of duty is getting stronger and stronger every day, telling him: "You are ready now, come then, open your sails to the wind and let it guide you. Never forget your past, draw your inspirations from it, and remember always: you are a son of Crete."

He dresses carefully, putting on the only suit he brought from Greece. He then puts on his tie and goes out. To his surprise, Samantha is right outside his building waiting to give him a ride.

She would like to keep this man in this country and to herself; she will do anything to achieve this. He will go back to Magdalene, though, and when that happens, she has to forget about him for good. Yet this faint sliver of hope flickers in her mind and doesn't allow her to let him go so easily.

"Hi, you look ready."

"Yes I am," he kisses her on her lips.

Samantha admires the way he looks; in the suit he is more handsome than ever. She also admires how far he has gone in just twenty months of hard work.

"I still can't believe you have completed your MBA in such a short time, Petros. I have to really congratulate you."

He laughs at her comment, and she sees a fine line of brushed white teeth.

Petros likes Samantha; she is just a fine gal and does everything for him: she found him a job, drives him around, listens to him, and most importantly, gives him the best sexual satisfaction he has ever experienced. That is why he has this slight desire to stay here and forget about going back home, yet he knows that the duty for him lies back in Greece, and the path he started some time ago.

Samantha embraces him happily and kisses him with passion. He pushes her away politely.

"We will be late. Let's go now."

"Alright then."

Petros looks in the mirror and fixes his tie one more time. Samantha starts the car and glances at him while she drives. She is upset by just thinking that soon he is going away, and she doesn't know whether she is going to ever see him again. When they are closer to the university, she takes the courage to go to the same subject she has been before:

"Tell me, Petros, what is after this degree? Are you really going to leave or will you consider staying and find a job someplace around here?"

He manages to answer with the same clarity and persistence: "You know I have to go, Sam. Why do you have to ask me again? I'm leaving as soon as I get a ticket. I have so much work to do back home."

"Magdalene is there also."

He nods his head without any comment.

"Isn't there anything to keep you here, Petros?"

"You don't have to ask that, sweetheart, because you know I could stay here, and you are the reason I could do this for, yet my call is so strong I cannot just forget everything I have planned all these years."

She leaves the subject alone, and by now they have reached the university grounds. She parks the car, and before he goes out she turns and takes his hand. She looks in his eyes and says.

"I'm going to come and visit you in Greece this coming summer."

"You are welcome to stay as long as you like. We'll have a great time together, I promise you."

She parks the car and they find the auditorium building.

"I'll wait for you in the cafeteria." Samantha says.

"Okay, I don't think it is going to be too long. I'll see you soon."

He goes to the auditorium and finds his way to his chair and sits. Everybody who needs to be there shows up slowly, and in a few minutes the place is packed. The professors arrive, along with all the dignitaries, and soon after, the ceremony starts. The speeches are the same as always. The graduates line up to receive their degrees accompanied by a hearty handshake from the dean and the professors of the faculty of economics. Petros Spathis' name is called, and he takes the paper (as he calls it), and shakes the hand of the dean who winks at him and smiles broadly. Then Petros returns to his seat, and soon enough, the whole thing is over. On his way out, his professor of the microeconomics class approaches him and says, "Spathis, I mean, Professor Spathis, I'd like to have a word with you."

Petros smiles back at the man who has been his teacher for two semesters.

"Well, I am not a professor quite yet, Professor, I would need a PhD for that, but I like the sound of it. What can I do for you?"

The man takes him by the arm and says, "Let us go to the cafeteria and have a drink; I'll tell you all about it."

Petros is more excited than surprised. He liked the sound of being called "Professor." They arrive at the cafeteria, where Petros spots Samantha in the corner. She sees him with his teacher and makes a gesture to ask what's going on. Petros shrugs his shoulders and motions to her to wait while he follows his teacher to a table.

"Spathis, do you remember once I asked you whether you were thinking of staying in this country? Well, I'm repeating the question today. The reason is that we have discussed your case and prepared to recommend to the school to offer you a good position here, as a teacher that is, if you can give us your word that you are to stay for at least three years."

Petros is caught unprepared. He is extremely pleased for what his teacher has said. He feels he can touch the sky if he gets up from his seat, and his face turns red. He hesitates at first to tell this fine man that his mind has been made up.

"If I'm to stay in this country for any reason, Professor, there wouldn't be any problem with me accepting this proposal. But I have made my decision, and I cannot see myself changing it now. I thank you and all the other members of the faculty very much for thinking so highly of me."

His teacher smiles and says regrettably, "I understand, although I'm very sorry for your decision not to stay. You will be an excellent teacher no matter where you go. I wish you the best in the future and never forget your time here."

With that comment he gets up and shakes Petros Spathis' hand once more and leaves.

"He offered me a teaching position in the school," he tells Sam.

"Now I can understand why he left so fast and with a sad face. You, of course, told him no."

"I didn't refuse the offer, Sam. I just told the man I want to go to my home country and teach."

"Stay, Petros, please stay! You will be very happy here with the teaching job and with me. We are going to be so happy."

She looks at him with adoration and waits for a positive reply.

He suddenly feels as if he is drowning, sinking, as if he cannot pick his feet up and walk away.

"Let's go somewhere," is all he can say.

They get into the car; she drives silently along 4th Avenue, then through Stanley Park, heading toward North Vancouver. Petros admires the huge cedar and fir trees and feels so close to nature. They drive over the famous Lions Gate Bridge and then take Highway 99 all the way up to Cypress Mountain. The car climbs uphill, and in a while they reach a beautiful vista point. She parks the car on the side of the road, and they get out. It is a cool afternoon. The water of the English Bay and the Lighthouse Park below is bright blue, and a couple of tug boats go slowly toward the harbor, hauling their barges filled with woodchips for the mill. Across the inlet, to the west of the city, is the Kitsilano neighborhood, and farther west is the university where they were not too long ago. He takes the courage to start the conversation on the same subject.

"Sam, please understand me. I must go back; I have a duty to fulfill. We have talked about this before, and you must know by now how I think and what I want in life. I can see that I may be able to have a happy life here without the uncertainties under the dictators, and all the rest of the garbage which comes along with my country, but that is where my duty lies, that is where I have a path waiting for me, and I have promised myself and all my family that I will go back. I can't see myself living here for good unless my life in Greece becomes so difficult and so miserable that I cannot function there anymore; perhaps then I may think of coming back here."

This is the first thread of hope he has given her.

"Petros, you don't need to say anything more. I think I know you well enough to understand what you want, what you are looking for, and what you want to fight against. Since there is no way I can convince you to change your mind, I have to tell you this: look around this beautiful place. I was born here; I grew up here. This is what I know, this is where I feel safe, and this is my home, same as Greece is your home. But, if you want me, I will give up all this for you. I can go to Greece with you and be with you for as long as you like. Petros, I'm willing to give up everything I have here if you just tell me, 'Yes, come with me, Samantha.' No don't say anything yet. Just think about what I told you, *Professor*."

With these last words she spreads her arms, showing him the beauty of the land below: the calm ocean, the mysterious trees, the smiling, glittering city—all harmoniously united. She imagines she is enclosing all of this in her hands, and she is prepared to give it all up for him.

Petros gently wipes away the tears on her cheeks and tries to to give her a sliver of sunshine.

"Thank you so much for trusting me so much, Sam. It makes me feel extremely guilty, but I have a gut feeling that I can't belong to any woman, at least not for now, and that is because I know the road I am going to take is not conventional, yet I must take it until the end. That's the only way it can be done. Please do not be angry with me. If for some reason I come back here, you are the one I'm going to be with no matter what, I promise."

"I'm afraid, Petros Spathis, that will never happen. I'm afraid something very bad is going to happen to you. Don't ask me how I know this; it is just a gut feeling, just as you called yours a minute ago. Be extra careful when you are back in Greece. All these things you are thinking of fighting, the ideals you believe in, they are part of a very dangerous game. You can never predict where these ideals will take you or what kind of people will be upset by you, and then it will be too late for you to leave. The end is very bitter most of the time, and it is predetermined by fate. So be careful, Petros Spathis, because you are going to get into a battle, and you can not foresee where it will take you. And, do take care of yourself, for me. I'm afraid that you will burn out before you have the chance to carry out any of your goals."

He is caught by surprise with her words, and feels a deep affection for her.

"Thank you, Sam, for your concern, but don't worry; everything is going to be fine. When you come to visit, you will see. Our lives do not depend just on our will but also on our destiny, it is something we cannot control."

His words come out so fast as if he had prepared them, yet his tone is convincing and earnest, and there is no pretense anywhere. She looks at him with affection,

"Okay, Petros, it is a date then. I will see you in three or four months in Greece."

"It is a date, Samantha. I'll be expecting you in Athens."

They get in the car and go back to town. She drops him off to his dorm room before she goes home.

The next morning, Petros Spathis goes to a travel agency and buys his ticket to Athens; he will be leaving in one week. He spends his last days clearing up the last of his affairs at school, his work at Ginno's, and medical and residential things. He also spends some time at the Greek Community and meets a few compatriots. He has had plenty of fun talking to these people who have made this country and this city their own home. He feels connected to these people because they have a strong, one-hundred-percent bond with their motherland after all this time in Canada. It is as if they have two homes, yet do not own either of them entirely.

The day of his departure comes, and Samantha drives him to YVR. They drop by Ginno's to say goodbye to her father, who Petros thanks for giving him the job and for his always kind words. Ginno is very sad to see him leaving and even sadder for his daughter. Yet, Ginno feels certain that time is the best healer in situations like this, so he reminds himself not to worry too much.

"Have a great trip and don't forget us, Petros."

"I won't, I promise."

Half an hour after Ginno's they arrive at the airport. Petros has his luggage checked and has about half an hour before he needs to go to his gate. So they wait together, and it's a dreadful thirty minutes for both of them. When it is time for him to go through the security check before his gate, Sam falls in his arms and kisses him passionately.

"Oh, Petros, Petros."

"Sam, thank you for everything. I will always cherish all the beautiful times we have had together. I'll be expecting you in the summer. Remember our date?"

"Yes, in four months, Petros. I'll see you."

He walks through the entrance to the security check, and then she can't see him anymore. He cannot see her tears, either.

After finding his seat on the aircraft, the plane soon takes off. Next stop is Frankfurt, and after that Athens. He falls into sleep and dreams he has already arrived.

8

Spring and summer have gone by, and the first days of September have arrived. Petros Spathis is a professor now at the University of Athens, the same school he graduated from two and a half years ago. He's in front of his office window staring outside before he goes to his class for the very first lecture. How time flies, he sighs. It seems everything only happened yesterday; all the experiences he has had the last two years, his trip to Vancouver, his life at the University of British Columbia, his return—all according to the plan he put together years ago, and it unfolds itself like the petals of a flower each morning with him taking the beauty out of every day as it comes.

Eleni, he found out, got married four months after he left the country, and now she is already expecting her first child. This is what she always wanted from him, too, but he was not able to give her, so she got her life started with another man. He wishes her well in his heart.

Magda was very excited when he got back; she came to the airport with his uncle and auntie to meet him. Yet, she still persisted that she wants him as her future husband. Now, under the pressure of his parents and Demetre and Maria, he has finally agreed to be engaged to her, but not until next spring at the earliest. Magdalene's father and mother like him; they have invited him to their home for dinner for the first time since he started to date her regularly. Even Magda's brother likes him. Still, Petros is not sure yet whether he is doing the right thing.

His uncle Demetre was so happy to see him return with his

master's degree that he went out of his way to buy Petros a mini cooper—1600 CCs, four cylinders, and a manual stick shift. Petros loves this car and washes it almost every day outside the apartment he now lives in on his own.

Today is his first lecture day, and he feels a bit uneasy. He has a clear idea about the subject he will develop in the course, what he will lecture for the first class, and at the first staff meeting his colleagues treated him very well as a newcomer and made him feel at home; however, he still wonders if the students will accept him.

He stands near the window looking at the traffic and the people on the boulevard. His thoughts go to Samantha who never made it to Greece in the summer, as she promised. She was working in full gear, busily involved with her dad's restaurant. She is good at keeping in touch, though, and that gives Petros the belief that she may indeed head his way some day. However, he won't know how to tell Magdalene if it happens and when it happens. Magda shows an amazing imagination and fright of him doing something she doesn't want him to do, like cheating on her. Her regular tirades of him being unfaithful annoys Petros so much that it makes him want to do exactly that just to justify her accusations.

Magdalene is her father's little princess who is spoiled to such a degree that she can be over conscious of herself and uncomfortably insecure. He has tried a number of times to tell her that he is not what she thinks of him, but her insecurity doesn't allow her to digest what she hears and the same tirade starts again and again.

The dean is supposed to come in a few minutes and introduce Petros to his first class as a new professor, but the dean is nowhere to be seen, adding to Petros' nervousness.

His thoughts are finally interrupted by the voice of the dean, "Come now, Spathis, let us go and teach these young men and women all they need to know, okay?"

"Thank you, Dean. I thought you forgot all about me."

He follows his boss down the hallway to his class. At the door before they enter, the dean turns and says, "Well, Spathis, are you ready?"

"Yes," he says firmly with a smile.

The students rise as Petros and the dean enter the classroom and the dean goes behind the podium and asks everyone to sit down. With Petros standing next to him, he begins quite formally, "My dear students, it is my great pleasure to introduce Professor Spathis to you. Professor Spathis steps into the class of economics upon a very careful selection of the senate. I hope you can share my joy and welcome him. I'm sure you will find he is a very good teacher, a good man and an excellent scholar."

He then turns to Petros, "Mr Spathis, I hope you will be satisfied working with these students, who are, I assure you, diligent and highly disciplined. Now I leave you to start your lecture."

He steps down from the podium.

"Thank you, Dean."

The dean goes out, and Spathis is alone with the fifty or so students and his TA, a woman named Amalia who he was introduced to earlier. He glances over the class: some of them seem to be even older than him.

"Ladies and gentlemen," he begins earnestly. Everyone is fully attentive to what he says. It gives him the courage to carry on for the rest of the hour, and soon the bell rings, telling him that his first and most dreadful hour has come to an end. He made it.

Over the next few days, he gets comfortable with how to run his classes and plan their curriculum. Then, he gets a surprise when the subject of the professor whom he replaced is brought forth in the class.

"I don't know what happened to your previous teacher," Petros says, "but I'm sure he was a very good teacher."

Antoniou, a man in his early thirties and one of the older students, strands up.

"They just fired him, Teacher. He was undesirable, if you know what I mean."

"Sorry, I don't. Why did he get fired, and who did that?"

"Because the junta didn't like what he preached to the class. They will probably do the same to anyone who stands in their way."

Petros does not expect himself to face this so soon, but he decides to make a stand and mark his ground right at this moment before it is too late.

"The junta is something not too many people like to have as a government, I know. But what can you do about it? Any ideas?"

The students stare at him, not having the courage to start the discussion. Fear is always the reason most people avoid doing anything against the government, and Petros can see fear on most of these students' faces, that is, except for Antoniou.

"What one can do, Teacher, is to get organized and kick them out," Antoniou's voice sounds calm.

"Now, that is an idea, yet how does one go about to do this?" Petros insists. "We can gather but it is against the law to start a people's movement."

This time, many students nod their heads. Professor Spathis is encouraged and tells his class that perhaps they can talk about this subject again at some other time.

More days go by, and his job becomes more comfortable for him, more beautiful and more meaningful. Slowly he finds out that a small group of his students are in regular contact with others from other faculties of the University of Athens and the city's polytechnic school who share the same political ideals. This gives him hope that sooner or later the junta is going to pay for all their prosecutions, imprisonments, beatings, and other violations of human rights they have committed against their own people in order to hold on to the power. He encourages them to carry on with their organizing and letter writing to newspapers in order for them to be ready for the appropriate time of action. He gets involved with the students council and their newspaper, something all other teachers avoid. These young students and their radical ideas may put somebody in danger of the wrath of the big politicos of Athens. However, Petros believes that the concerns of the students are the concerns of all Greeks, and it is his duty to help them the best he can.

One day after the lecture, a group of students surround him in the hallway and ask him about some pressing problems related to the freedom of speech. He tries to help them develop their ideas and bring forward the necessary solutions. These young men are so tense and wounded by the junta's strict media regulations; Petros sympathizes with them but knows the real solutions are still far away. As long as the junta controls the mass media and has a political observer stationed in every university faculty, none of the students, or teachers for that matter, can do or say much. He promises to take their concerns to his colleagues and see whether any of the professors can get involved or give them the proper attention. His students are delighted to know that they can count on this new teacher for support.

The dean appears from the other side of the hallway and walks toward Petros who is surrounded by the students. The dean smiles, "Hello Spathis, I was looking for you. I didn't find you in your office."

"Hi, Dean," Petros smiles then turns to the students and says, "all right, we'll carry on with this some other time. Good day to all."

"Students, you know," the dean says as they walk away together.

"I know, I know," says Petros. "They are admirable, aren't they?"

The dean leads the way to his big office, and when they enter, he comes right to the point,

"Spathis, I must warn you that you are taking the students' demands much too seriously. These matters have been going on for quite some time already. You must bear in mind that even the walls have ears, and there are certain people who just don't like to be disturbed. Listen to what I'm trying to tell you. Most of the time these kids do not know what they want, and then they want everything in one day. Things cannot change within one day; you should understand this better than they do. You simply have to distance yourself from them, stick to your lectures, and leave the politics to the politicians. I am alarmed when hearing comments from the junta. You know very well they keep an eye on us. You also know very well they canned your predecessor much too early in his career."

The dean gives his imposing talk in one breath and looks into

Petros' eyes imperiously, leaving no room for objections. Petros realizes that it is better for him to just nod his head, but he feels it is his duty to try to win the dean to his side. He explains to the dean about his beliefs in freedoms and rights, and that the junta should not dictate the rules and punish the offenders. Yet, the dean is not someone who can be easily influenced.

"Spathis, I, for one, doubt the righteousness of the manner in which you conduct your work when it comes to the students. You pay too much attention, or better yet, you give too much encouragement, or rather, freedom to your students. This is why they have the guts to come out straight and criticize the government. This is why they feel they have you as an ally when time comes; they use your position to help them achieve their goals."

"What are their goals then, Dean?" Petros dares to interrupt.

"You pay too much attention to what they think, and that is a mistake. You must not be so sensitive to their demands. These kids think that they already know everything about life, but I assure you they know absolutely nothing. They are still too young and immature to be able to impose their views of things on us. You know."

Petros Spathis is now angry and does not make any effort to hide it from his boss,

"I'm sorry I don't agree with you here, Dean. These 'kids', as you refer to them, are not kids at all; they are young, mature, and upright women and men. Some of them may not have enough life experiences, but that does not mean that they lack the ability to think and find ideal solutions to what concerns them and their lives in school. They also show a very deep understanding of the need for political changes in this country. They are not kids; they are young citizens who have every right that we have, although these rights have been suppressed so much the last few years, thanks to the politicos and the dictators."

The dean feels his temples pounding, his face is hot,

"Spathis, in a way you are right, but as the time goes by, you'll find out for yourself that often these thoughts, these ideals, and this attention you pay to them may prove to be too destructive for you to handle because those people you are pointing finger at have power to destroy a person's life very easily. I can only tell you to be very careful, be very careful. Even the walls have ears these days."

"Yes, of course, you are right, Dean. Thank you very much for your advice," Petros says, sensing that the dean is too stubborn to be persuaded in this debate. Just before Petros turns to leave, the dean says, "Oh, I almost forgot. I would like you to come to my house later on tonight for a cup of coffee. Can you make it?" The dean senses that the invitation sounds more like a command, so he tries to lighten it up: "My wife likes very much the idea of meeting with your girlfriend. Are you already engaged, Spathis?"

"Not yet, but we plan to this in the spring. Thank you for asking, Dean. What time would you like us to be there?"

"Any time around eight o'clock."

"Alright, thanks again. See you later."

Petros goes out of the dean's office, angry with himself and his boss. In the elevator, he presses the button furiously and waits. The car comes, the door slides open, and he comes face to face with his TA, Amalia.

"Oh, hi," she says. "I've been looking for you."

"Why? Do you need anything, Amalia? It seems everyone is looking for me today. The dean just finished talking with me."

"It looks like your meeting with him has caused you some distress."

"Yes, he is so stubborn with the protocol," he says, trying not to get into details.

"Well, what I need to know is what subject you are going to explore today. We are due in class in ten minutes. Last time you promised the students to discuss the taxation system, if you recall."

All of a sudden, Petros doesn't feel like teaching today.

"Yes, but today I need to take some time off to attend to a personal matter, so can you tutor the class? Perhaps a review of the last two lectures," he says and readies himself to go.

She is taken by surprise, as he has never missed a class for any reason up to now. She thinks that the dean must have gotten him very upset.

"Well that is just fine, Petros. I'll see you tomorrow then."

"Yes, tomorrow. Good day, Amalia."

"Good day to you too."

He leaves quickly, with his eyes filled with disappointment.

Amalia is left in the elevator alone with her own disappointment, thinking of her lack of courage. She has been his assistant since the beginning of the semester and as the days have gone by she has more and more feelings for him. She loves to be in the classroom with Petros, observing and admiring him as he lectures and discusses topics with the students. She loves the confident manner. Her joy is even greater when she is in his office, and they talk about all kinds of issues together, giving her the chance to intimately connect with him. Can she be in love with him? She shivers. She doesn't try to answer herself because she already knows. But what can be the outcome of something like this? He is to be married to this girl who comes from a very rich and well-positioned family. He looks quite happy with Magdalene whenever she sees them together. Amalia's elderly parents are eagerly waiting for her to settle down. Her family, her friends, her childhood spent in a poor neighborhood—all these demand that she marries and lives an honest and moral life. But things haven't turned out as she has expected; she is in love with Professor Petros Spathis.

She looks at her watch. She has to go to the class. She takes out her clipboard and a piece of paper and prepares a rough outline of her lecture as she walks briskly through the corridors.

The same evening, Petros drives his car to Magda's house and picks her up for their visit at the dean's house. It is busy out on the streets; the noise and commotion are at their peak. Petros stops the car at a red light, observing the passersby who make their way across the intersection in front of them—a crowd of men and women, boys and girls of all types: tall, short, blond, dark-haired, thin, fat, some going this direction, others the opposite; but all are trying to push their way through to their destinations, like sheep following the whistle of a shepherd.

The light changes, but Petros is still lost in his thoughts. Magda pokes his shoulder to alert him, and he starts pressing the gas pedal.

"I'm sorry, Magda, I almost fell asleep," he lies, feeling guilty for leaving her out of his thoughts. He feels so much for Magda, and he knows she feels the same for him. Yet, at times he knows he neglects her by being so enclosed to his own world, a place which he rarely lets her in. He turns his head to look at her. She is extremely beautiful tonight. He takes her hand affectionately, as if he were a high-school boy falling in love for the first time. This girl is going to be his wife. Her graceful appearance, her black, straight hair wound tight on the back of her head, her graceful neckline, her eyes, her ways, her aristocratic flair, her always calm and polite manners—all these are part of his Magda, including her spoiled childhood whims that can challenge his patience at times. She is soon going to be his wife, and he is terribly in love with her.

They arrive at the dean's residence, and Petros rings the doorbell. The host appears at the entrance and welcomes them warmly. He guides them to the living room where they see three women and two men. Petros recognizes the dean's wife.

"My dear friends," says the dean, "may I present you with Mr Spathis and his fiancée Magdalene." The dean then turns to Petros and Magda. "And this is Colonel Stathis Vikas and Mrs Vikas, Colonel Prodromos Alvarezos and Mrs Alvarezos."

Petros and Magda shake hands with each of them, exchanging polite greetings. When Petros is shaking Alvarezos' hand, the dean tells him in a boasting tone, "Colonel Alvarezos is the government trustee in our school. You have probably heard of him."

Petros tries to keep his self-control. Had he known that Alvarezos would be there tonight, he would not have come; he has heard a few monstrous stories about the junta's eyes and ears at the school. His blood runs hot in his veins, rises to his head, and almost chokes him. He fights hard not to show his feelings although he cannot hide it from Magda who leans closer to him and looks at him with puzzling eyes. He says nothing to her.

"Well Spathis, how do you like your work at the university?" asks Vikas with a warm smile.

The dean hurries to interject, "I'm sure he is quite satisfied with his work."

Petros laughs and adds, "The dean is right, Colonel. The job suits me well, and I try my best to fulfill my responsibilities. There are, of course, certain problems as in any job, although to some people these problems appear negligent."

"What kind of problems?" Vikas asks.

"Our young people, I believe, are superior to all other young people in the world, Colonel. They have many virtues, and they are very curious. They like research, inquiring, and earnest discussions. They solve problems independently or by working them out among themselves. They are becoming true scholars. I am there primarily to give them extra facts which they have not picked up on their own, and make them aware of simple, rational, and modern methods. Yes, on the whole, I'm completely satisfied with my students. But, of course, they have certain demands as well. I feel frustrated because I cannot fully be of service to their education as the situation is hard these days."

"What do you mean the situation is hard, Spathis?" Alvarezos asks immediately.

"The students are not happy with the restrictions the administration puts on them; they are also dissatisfied with the political situation in the country, the freedoms and rights of the people, things like that. They want to see changes for the immediate future. There are times when I try to give them a bright side to look at, yet they always resist these halfway measures, wanting a complete change in direction from both the administration of the school and the government in general."

"Do you think they are right in those demands, Spathis?" the government trustee asks, but quickly adds, "Yet, it is impossible for these kids to understand the reasons for the 'restrictions', as you choose to call them."

Petros is now really annoyed and says, "Are you suggesting that those things you do to violate the freedoms and rights of the students and the general population are not restrictions? This is the country where democracy was introduced to the world. Now we are not living in a democratic system. I don't know what you call this 'government', Mr Alvarezos, but I call it a dictatorship."

Vikas, fearing the worst from the government trustee, rushes to intervene, "Yes, Spathis, you are right, but don't forget the instability and chaos here before the army intervened. It wasn't democracy at all, I'm sure you remember."

"Yes, Colonel, I agree. However, that is the price of democracy and the way to higher civilization. If this was what the country had to go through in order for it to find its way, let be so. Look at Italy: they have changed the government every two years since the Second World War. On the other hand here, think of what price our people have paid the last six years: all these undesirables whom the junta has arrested and put away with this excuse and that excuse? What about all those people? Are they not members of our society? They are put away without due process, without any justification other than the most brainless excuse of 'national security' and that sort of crap."

Now Petros is furious. He feels this is the historic time in his life when he can put a stamp on the cheek of life and make it stay there forever.

All the guests are speechless. Magda is quite pleased at his comments. She smiles at him admiringly, giving him her approval. The dean's face turns red; he doesn't know how the school trustee is going to react and what is going to happen tomorrow at the office. Vikas is the only one who has a faint smile on his face, not trying to hide it from anybody.

Petros, seeing Magda agreeing with him, carries on,

"Personally, I see all the restrictions of the administration as nothing more than militarizing our school system. Undercover policemen and military officers are in the lecture rooms, for God's sake. Do you think that my students or I haven't noticed them? Do you think that the students feel free to speak when they see these guys spying on everyone? Of course you can say this is a period of adjustment. The question is how long will this adjustment take? We are already in the sixth year under the military rule. How much longer? It only creates fear and nothing else. There is no real reason anymore for this government to exist. It would be better if they just decide to walk away. Let people choose their leaders as they have the right to."

Petros suddenly notices the effect of his speech on people. The dean is speechless, his face bloated like a carnival mask, when Petros looks at him he wants to laugh but manages to control himself. Alvarezos is nervously tapping his fingers on the armchair. The women stand apart from their husbands, watching Petros intensely. Only Colonel Vikas is still calm, smiling with certain admiration and understanding.

The scene is interrupted by the hostess, who serves them coffee and dessert.

The dean somewhat calms down, making a futile effort to draw the attention away from the debate: "How about some music?"

Nobody takes notice of his question. Alvarezos continues to eye the new teacher with hostile eyes, and queries, "So these are your views of our current situation, Spathis?"

"Yes, of course. Let us leave the students on the side. Do you think that the teachers and the TAs feel comfortable lecturing under the watchful eye of the big brother, knowing all the time that they may be misunderstood by the officials who are hardly educated enough to follow half of what is said? For example, what happened to the teacher who had the position I occupy now? Apparently, the official word is that he 'resigned'. But why would an excellent scholar like him leave this university? He didn't resign; he was simply canned for his beliefs. All of you know that, as all the students do as well."

The dean tries to intervene again, "There were reasons to why he resigned, Spathis."

"Yet he did not resign, Dean. He was fired because the peons of the junta got something he said the wrong way. Do not insist in telling me he resigned, please; you may even make me believe it," Petros' voice is harsh and sarcastic as he spoke this last sentence, which silences the dean.

Petros feels a little guilty, so he tries to move attention away from him, "What is your opinion, Colonel Vikas?"

Vikas, who has been listening closely to their exchange, is startled. He sits up in his chair and responds, "Spathis, my view is divided between yours and Alvarezos'. It is true that many irregularities exist in the whole administrative and political set up, but do not forget that this is a temporary stage we are going through. Sooner or later it will come to an end. Besides, in certain situations we do err in our decisions, but all people make mistakes; the intellectual level of the populace is simply not high enough to avoid making mistakes. Mistakes, Spathis, are a fact of life. Previous governments made them, and they cannot be excluded altogether from the present government, although the necessity for change is evident."

Vikas speaks calmly, emphasizing every word. Petros, as an intelligent observer, detects a note of hope.

"Undoubtedly, Colonel, everybody makes errors, but let me add something to your point of the intellectual level of the populace. How can that change if all the efforts of the teachers turn futile? Look at our government: because of the hunger for money, they import the cheapest goods and materials and without any concern of the people's needs whatsoever, just as long as the government has a chance to make money. Look at how we encourage our populace to spend their leisure time: we give them a soccer game to get them out of our sight. Look at the ways we administer the procedure of lotteries. Look at what we do with our medical system. Look at our employment system ... We are in the sixth year of the revolution. What have they achieved? Allow me to answer: hardly anything. The same is going on as before. If the government wants to call its movement a revolution, show us the changes. If they claim that doing this is for the betterment of the populace, release all wrongly imprisoned people and leave them alone to live their lives without the fear of punishment for what they believe in. Here you have it, Colonels Vikas and Alvarezos. Give people what they should have: freedom. When you do so, I'll then accept this 'revolution', as you call it. Don't forget there are so many hungry people in our society because they cannot find a job; so many sick people who cannot afford a treatment because they do not have medical coverage; and so many uneducated because they are not given the chance to go to school. What's worst: there are so many people who still don't have electricity to light their houses or roads to connect them to a civic center. Yet our government has so far only pretended to know how to take care of the populace. No, we don't need dictatorships; we need a government which truly cares for their citizens. Simple."

Petros feels so relieved; he has spoken out and with passion; his mark has been made on the skin of the day, and his path is drawn clearly in front of these three men.

"What can be done, Colonels?" Petros continues. "Also, when can we get rid of a system of political connections? You know inequalities can be found whenever one is out there looking for employment. Whom you know is always the key rather than how you are qualified for the job. This is most unfortunate."

Petros Spathis stops for a minute and looks at the others, one by one, searching for any reaction, any counter argument; but he is right about their being apathetic. The dean is staring at the chandelier in the room rather intensely, as though he saw it for the first time. Alvarezos sips his coffee slowly, staring into the flames of the fireplace. Colonel Vikas is the only one who is still turned to Professor Spathis. Vikas' forehead is lined with wrinkles, his eyebrows are raised, and eyes focus on Petros. He makes a gesture with his hand as though he'd like to say something but then changes his mind.

At last, the dean turns back to Petros, "All these things, Spathis, I believe are common in most countries. We must not think of them as peculiar to our nation alone. There are, of course, situations which are in need of change; but sometimes it is more dangerous to expose them than to accept them."

"Well, well, now the dean is changing his tune," Petros muses. "He still disagrees with me, but this time he is defensive, hesitant. It is as though he is trying to tell me that if we were in some other place, or better, if we were alone, he could accept everything I have said up to now."

With new courage, Petros feels compelled to carry on even more forcefully than before.

"You may be right, Dean, maybe most of these problems do exist in other countries, but it doesn't mean we have to put up with them at all. Besides, we are always proud that we gave civilization to the world through the philosophy and the arts of our ancestors. Let us set a good example for others to imitate. We must begin at some point, gentlemen, and there is no more appropriate time than today. The present government, with all its revolutionary characteristics, should also be the most capable body to effect the proper changes. A revolution's first duty is to bring equality and civil rights to its people. So let us start again with a new beginning to reshape the future of this country and be the example. If we really want revolution and like to say goodbye to the instabilities, let us give the people the chance to elect their leaders as they are supposed to do in any democracy and turn this country into a new institution; let us give the political prisoners their rights back and help this country to establish new rules to free people rather than oppress them; let us do the right thing for the betterment of the populace. True revolution always depends on continuous changes."

Petros Spathis completes his speech and feels at ease enough to stretch comfortably in his seat and sip his coffee. He brings his glance to Magda who is staring at him. He motions to her discreetly, and she responds by moving her eyebrows. She looks a little sad.

The clock ticks and all four men remain silent, each one drawn into their own thoughts. They look like opponents in a game, who stop once in a while to check one another out, to measure each other's strength. Alvarezos is eyeing Petros darkly, like the inquisitor of a past era, and thinks that this young professor is a very powerful orator. If he joins any political party or is simply out on the streets talking to common masses, he is likely to become one of those men who can incite a political movement. Perhaps at a different time he may even like this young professor; he may even joint him for some common cause. But now is a dangerous time. Will Petros Spathis have a chance to talk to the general populace about his ideas? Can the university afford to have him amongst the easily influenced young students? Alvarezos can't help but wonder about the worst-case scenario. He concludes that this young professor is indeed dangerous, and he has to do something about him soon. He shudders; the thought of "doing something" to Petros Spathis scares him. Inside him two different worlds are at war, two opposite, irreconcilable worlds. He knows he is doomed to be tormented by them just like Odysseus fighting with the two wild beasts, and it will be difficult for him to find peace. Petros does not know that twenty-six years of army life has taken its toll on Alvarezos' dreams of becoming a lawyer and fighting for justice with his words, only words, not violence. This dream is now an old memory filled with nostalgia and tenderness in difficult moments like this one and when he is to submerge into the labyrinth of the articles and paragraphs, notes, and footnotes of the army regulations. He envies Spathis in a way; actually, he is jealous of him, and anybody who has the guts to state his opinion and be free to believe in what his heart tells him is right.

Alvarezos manages to calm his racing mind. The storm of his soul has subsided, and for a moment it is quiet and sunny. But then it becomes dark again; the sun disappears behind the gray clouds and the sea becomes stormy under the wind, which has once again started to blow, forcefully and violently. It stings his body and turns him into a different man.

He turns to the dean as if he was a ruler speaking to his slave, "And you, Dean, what is your opinion of all what Spathis said?"

Alvarezos pronounced "Dean" very explicitly, and sarcastically. He continues to tap his fingers on the arm of the chair with a rhythmic military like beat. At this moment his resentment for the army floods him. He is now nothing more than an obedient zombie to the rules; he is a well-sprung machine, ready to move mechanically according to the demands of some superior.

The dean is surprised at his unexpected question and feels as though someone poured cold water over him. What will the dean say? Petros looks at him questionably. Vikas too.

"Colonel Alvarezos," the dean starts, "there are certain things about which Spathis is completely right. Of course, no one can deny the fact that we are at fault sometimes in terms of human rights, especially when we don't try to correct this problem. But in other respects, I disagree with Spathis. For example, I don't believe people are pushed into things. I do not view the propaganda in the same light as he does. Besides, I don't believe that there are scholars who are pushed to the side for political reasons as Spathis suggests."

The dean exhales in relief seeing the approval on the trustee's face. Petros looks at both of them and wonders why the dean is so afraid to utter the truth. Is he so weak that he cannot face it? Is he so brainwashed that he cannot see the truth even if it is one inch in front of his eyes?

Colonel Vikas gets up from his chair, places his hands behinds his back, and goes to stand in front of the fireplace. Petros is encouraged by this move and anticipates that Vikas is about to have a speech.

The colonel starts as if he addressing new recruits: "Let us remember, gentlemen that we need to retain our objectivity and see things the way they really are. That being said let us also not be concerned with the ideal world. In general terms, I have to agree with Petros, almost totally in fact. Yes, we are the reason why there are people who are neglected, suppressed, persecuted. We are the reason why a lot of our citizens are in jails. I do believe, truly believe, though, that this is a temporary problem, and soon we'll have things moving in the right direction, toward a new kind of democracy that all other countries will be envious of. Yes, we push our populace to the wrong direction at times, but we will correct these mistakes. We need to start seeing the well being of our citizens with a different eye than before. We need to put aside the greed for money and provide the needy with proper facilities, means, medical coverage, and all the rest. Of course this will take time, but I truly believe, I repeat myself, I truly believe we shall come to this slowly as the days and years go by. There are times that even I hate the way things are done, and even the work I do, but it is the work I have learned to do, and I cannot start something new at my age. As a matter of fact, I'm thinking of leaving my post at some time in the near future."

Alvarezos is enraged to hear him talking like that and taking the young professor's side: *What is wrong with those people?* he thinks. They don't know where they belong to, and they always bite the hand that feeds them. He knows that to take out the young teacher is going to be a piece of cake, but to take out one of their own is something the party machine has to ponder for some time. After all, this colonel is being around for so long and has paid his dues to the cause, to the country, to everyone. Who can really put all that aside and order his demise? Yet, there is only one way a government can stay in power, Alvarezos is certain, and that is only if they take out their opponents; everybody knows that. He starts devising a scheme in his mind which he can recommend to the echelons above him. He turns to face another direction, away from Vikas, who carries on with a few more ideas. In a way Alvarezos admires Colonel Vikas for speaking his truth just as Petros Spathis, but people like these two are not suitable to be free to roam the streets in these extra difficult times.

The dean looks at Vikas and wonders who this man really is. Is he crazy? What is going to happen to the school and the students and the young professor? Is Spathis going to end up like the previous teacher? The dean even starts to question whether his own future is at risk. After all, he is the one who invited both these men to his house. Do people like Vikas and Spathis really think they can act in this way without consequences?

Alvarezos knows Vikas spent his early years in the service during the war against the Germans and was awarded the cross of valor. How does a man like him turn out to be so different now that he has aged? Alvarezos continues to tap his fingers rhythmically on the arm of his chair, but his face shows inexplicable calmness—the storm has just gone by his heart and his mind, and now the peace brought by his plan of getting rid of these two somehow graces him with an unexpected serenity.

There are times even Alvarezos hates his job and the protocol, but the difference is that Vikas has the courage to admit it and deal with the pain involved. Alvarezos simply does not have the courage to face his own fear of doing something beyond the black book of conduct and the regulations. It is impossible for him to break the bonds and fight for the truth without fear of punishment. He has to hang onto the ropes even though he doesn't even believe in his position. He looks at the young professor who is still admiring Vikas, at the dean who is still red in the face, and at Vikas who has great pride in his eyes. "Gentlemen," Alvarezos says as he gets up. "It is time for us to go," he nods to everybody and traces his steps to the door along with his wife.

After the door closes behind Alvarezos and his wife, Magda steps closer to the men: "I wonder all the problems have been solved or not, Dean?"

"If not all, then most of them, my dear," he manages to answer in the same cheerful manner.

They all get ready to go. Petros and Vikas exchange telephone numbers as they promise one another to meet again soon.

9

A few days go by without any incident, and Petros Spathis is busy with his work and the students. He has spent quite some time with Antoniou and a few others, and they slowly develop an understanding that something has to be done. Antoniou has the idea of preparing certain pamphlets about civil disobedience and having them distributed to the students of other faculties. Hopefully, this small flame will soon turn into a wildfire to engulf all the oppression in Athens and the rest of Greece.

Toward the end of September, Petros gets a call from Colonel Vikas who invites him and Magda to go fishing near his summer home in a village northeast of Athens called Kalamos, about one hour's drive away by car. Petros gladly accepts the invitation. "Great, I will pick you up tomorrow morning at eight o'clock then," Vikas says cheerfully. Petros tells Magda of the invitation, but she is not really interested in the idea, so he decides to go on his own.

Vikas arrives right at eight a.m.

"Good morning, Petros."

"Good morning, Vikas."

They shake hands and are on their way. In a short while they are out of the city. It is a beautiful day: the air is crystal clear and fresh. It is a little chilly, but very soon when the sun is up higher, the heat of September becomes quite comfortable.

"You see, Petros, the weather is on our side today."

"I see that. By the way, I assume you have all necessary gear for fishing today?"

"Of course, Anagnostis the villa keeper has already put together what we need for the day. I phoned him yesterday."

"I love traveling to this side of the country. This is our country, Vikas, and we have to make it the best there is for everyone to enjoy," Petros says with a passion and his eyes are encompassing the whole countryside.

Vikas nods and they start to chit chat about more things. Shortly, they arrive at his villa. There is a gate with the name "Villa Elena" on it, and Vikas drives along the driveway to the front entrance. He puts the car on the side and asks Petros to follow him inside.

Petros is enchanted by the sight of the construction. It is a superb house, perfectly designed in an old style, aristocratic, and yet in such a manner that one cannot call it old fashioned. When inside, Vikas pulls the curtains aside, and the sun fills the main room with light. Obviously a man of style and class, he proudly shows Petros around. The walls are full of nice paintings, some very famous. Above the fireplace, two shotguns are displayed, with their barrels facing one another. On the opposite wall hang many hunting trophies and swords crafted in silver with handcrafted handles. A huge bookcase covers one wall of the room with a big desk, two chairs, and a couch. On the other side of the room rests a piano, an old radio, and a stereo set. Down two or three steps is a dining room with a stairway in the corner that leads to the bedrooms. Near the stairway stands a glass tank with well-selected collection of fish and sea life.

Vikas prepares a coffee for both of them, and goes outside to find where Anagnostis put the fishing gear. After a short while, he comes back inside, his face pleased, and takes Petros out to his "kingdom": the basement where there are all kinds of wines in a cellar, a billiard table, and a table tennis. Petros is amazed. It is a beautiful place.

"I see you are a billiards fan too, hey?" Petros says excitedly.

"Great, perhaps we can have a game sometime," Vikas laughs, "perhaps after our fishing expedition."

"Agreed."

"Your villa is just fantastic, Vikas," Petros repeats a comment he has made earlier.

"Thank you, Petros. But let us get going. I'm sure the fish are getting impatient."

The sun, high in the sky now, sends them its warm greetings. The serenity is disturbed only by the noise of their footsteps on the gravel road to the seashore. When getting to the boat, they find all the fishing rods, lines and hooks, and in a small bag shrimp for them to use as bait. Vikas starts the motor, and the boat leaves a small wave on their way out. The sea is unusually hospitable this morning and in a short while they are about half a kilometer away from the land. They stop and Vikas puts down the small anchor. Petros can't help admiring him: this is a man who knows what he wants to do in life, a man who has found his balance between nature and his work.

"Alright. Here is where we try our luck. Get your rod and try this bait; see what happens," Vikas tells Petros and gets the other fishing rod for himself.

Petros gets his stuff ready and in less than a minute casts his line.

"You think that I know nothing about fishing, Colonel? Watch me get the first one. By the way, what do we expect to catch here?"

"There are quite a few perch around this bottom. I have caught them a number of times," Vikas answers. Then he adds, "I would like to give you some recent news first."

"Yes, Colonel, what is it?"

"I suspect that something has been done behind my back, and I believe it has to do with you as well. That pig, Alvarezos, knows a lot of people, and those people nowadays pull all the strings. You know he is an officer of the A2, right? The intelligence agency carries more weight than the army's artillery unit where I belong. This is why I want to warn you: be careful. You spoke so openly the other night at the dean's home; it worries me a lot. I know they cannot do anything to me; I am at a stage of my career that I can leave anytime, and they don't necessarily need me anymore. But for you, your future is threatened now, and your life may be in danger."

"But Vikas, I haven't said anything wrong, I haven't done anything wrong, and I don't intend to do anything wrong in the future. Why would I worry about the junta that much? I'm sure they have other more important things to do, like governing the country and producing some positive results for the people."

"Look, I agree with you. I see how wholeheartedly you believe in your views, but these animals only care for the power and how to stay in power. I'm quite certain they have bugged your office and the class where you conduct your lectures, and I'm also concerned they have put their own spies in the students associations. Be careful. Every word you say they can hear, every move you make they can see, and every person you meet they can take away and interrogate. This is a very bad situation we are in, and you have to be patient until all this changes."

Petros Spathis shakes his head and can't believe what he has heard, yet deep inside he knows the man's reasoning is as clear as the sunshine. There must be a serious reason why he is taking this risk to tell him all this information.

"Thank you, Vikas. Nothing really surprises me. But I intend to stick around and do my job and hope for the best."

His voice is steady and his eyes bright like the sky. He looks at Vikas gratefully, knowing he and this man are bonded, and that the colonel will never stop short of doing what is best.

Suddenly he feels a tugging at his line, so he reels it in as fast as he can. Finally he brings up a nice size porgy, beating violently at the other side of the line.

"Well, bravo, Petros. You got the first one. Good job."

They both grin.

Petros' glance goes far out to the open sea, where a ship is visible. It carves a path through the water into the unknown. Suddenly he feels that strange shudder again, which makes him worry.

The month of October comes with its usual rain, and the cold spells just follow one after the other. Petros keeps busy at school, and he notices his TA, Amalia, is interested in him more than just being her professor. A number of times he catches her eyes fixating on him longer than usual, her hands accidentally touching his when the opportunity arises. She also passes her tongue over her lips really close to his face when they discuss things. He receives a call from Samantha and realizes she is on her way to Athens six days from now. He is a bit excited for her courage to take this long trip, although he knows Magdalene is not going to like it at all, but, then again, he has not seen her since the dinner at the dean's house.

   The city takes on its usual rhythm. Today, Petros gets up early to prepare himself for the lecture scheduled for nine o'clock. On his way to school, which is a twenty-minute drive, he pays attention to the 'mood of the city' as he calls it, how the day unfolds in front of his eyes. People seem to go to places as they always do. The late risers and casual pedestrians are not around yet. The October sun is full of optimism as it rises behind the Penteli Mountain: there isn't a cloud to be seen in the sky. The highrise buildings stand one beside the other, gracing the city with certain nobility. The streets, which will only see the sun later in the day, still retain the damp chill of a fall morning. The housewives are already hanging the bed sheets and other laundry on the balcony railings to freshen them in the morning breeze, and having the chance to gossip from one balcony to another. The news of what happens in the neighborhood usually circulates at this time every morning.

   He drives his car, and he senses he does so with a certain roughness, certain anger, and he questions himself why he feels this way this particular morning. What is he to do with Samantha? Is he going to accommodate her in his apartment, or let her go and get a hotel? If he takes her to his place, Magda is not going to like it at all, he knows. Yet Sam and her dad helped him so much when he was in Vancouver; he feels obligated to help her out now that he has the chance. The car in front of him stops suddenly, and he applies the brakes accordingly. There is some construction going on the side of the street, and a dumptruck is unloading a truckload of gravel. He puts his head out of the window and watches the construction workers do their job.

   Distracted by the workers, he forgets to see the green light until the car behind him honks. He starts again and soon arrives at the school. He goes to the cafeteria first to order a coffee and asks the server to bring the coffee to his office.

"Good morning Petros."

Amalia is in his office already.

"Good morning, Amalia. What do we have to look at today?"

His voice hints certain indifference, which he intends to show her most of the times in their daily interactions. She reads that well. Disappointed, she bites her lower lip. Petros notices her reaction and feels a little guilty, so he tries to correct the situation; after all, this is a pretty twenty-five year old woman with an excellent figure, and Petros has a weak spot for girls like her. Her pretty eyes are hidden behind her glasses, and he finds her more sensual when he is close to her. He knows if he makes a move, she is going to respond positively . . .

"I see you are here quite early today. Why?" he teases her and the funny tone puts a smile on her immediately.

"And you Petros, why are here so early?" she answers in the same way.

"Perhaps I'm here to spend some time with my pretty assistant before the lecture," he moves closer to her.

He touches her lips with his index finger, and a moment later they are kissing. He takes her glasses off; yeah, really, she is a very pretty young woman. He enjoys the taste of her lips and her tongue. Not too long after, they are both sexually aroused; however, he is not ready yet to lay her on his desk, and he pushes her to go down on him, an act which she does with so much pleasure and fervor that it only takes him a couple of minutes to come right there in her mouth. She gets up quickly, and runs to his bathroom, and he hears her having a hard time trying to vomit as hard as she can. It is obvious that this is the very first time she has tasted it. He smiles at the thought that neither Samantha nor Magdalene ever had the same problem. When she comes out of the bathroom, he says apologetically, "I'm sorry if I put you on the spot."

She smiles faintly without saying anything, putting her glasses back on. They carry on with the preparation for the lecture.

A few days go by and Petros enjoys the routine of things until the day comes when Sam is due to arrive. He goes to his office and meets with Antoniou and a couple of other students for half an hour. Amalia is with them as well. They arrange to go to his place two nights from now with all the pamphlets prepared so he can peruse them and give his okay before distributing them to other schools. Later in the afternoon he tells Amalia that he has to leave early because he has to pick up a friend from the airport.

Samantha's flight will arrive at about four-thirty, and he has a couple of hours to kill. He wants to be alone for a while and ponder what to do with this group of young men and their ideas of a civil disobedience scheme. It worked years ago in India during the Gandhi days; why not here?

He drives his car, taking the direction to the seashore. Soon he leaves the city behind and reaches the last road before the beach. He parks the car on the side of the road and gets out. He stands by the road looking at the blue sea of the Gulf of Piraeus. He finds a narrow trail leading to the water and follows it until he steps on the beach. There are many rocks there, and he sits on a relatively big one, not caring whether it is clean or dirty. He gazes at the open water. After a while, he gets up and starts walking. He tries to jump form one rock to another until he gets tired and stops. A small crab catches his eye: it is sunbathing. He picks it up. The crab moves his legs rapidly, but Petros has a good grip on him. The crab struggles more, and Petros holds it tighter. Suddenly Petros sees himself in this crab, caught by a mighty hand, and he knows he cannot escape from such a grip. He will use all his strength to free himself just as the crab in his hand, yet the unknown power will not let go as easily as he does when he releases it. The crab runs to its hideout. He is mesmerized when seeing how fast this crab makes it to the dark side of the rock and away from his sight. The strongest instinct of survival, that superb gift of nature, is guiding the crab to where the safest place is. But where can Petros Spathis go? Will he hide behind some securely established place? He bends down and wets his face with the cold, crystal-like water. It makes him feel better. He looks again at the open sea and the seagulls with their horrible screeching as they fly close by.

He follows the trail back to his car then makes his way to the airport. When he arrives, there is still some time left before Samantha's flight is scheduled to arrive, so he finds a bar to sit down and enjoy a light lunch with a good cup of coffee. Finishing his food, he goes to the arrivals gate and there she comes, full of smiles and excitement. She falls in his arms, and they kiss passionately. He knows he cannot ask her to go to a hotel. She is here to visit him, whether Magda likes it or not. He tells himself that this may be another way to get Magda a bit away from him. Somehow he knows the black clouds will eventually come closer, and the insanity of the system will catch up with him. When that happens, he doesn't like to have anybody around him.

"Welcome to Athens, Sam," he hugs Samantha who looks so pretty in her light green jacket and her sexy tight pants outlining a well-rounded behind he loves to play with.

"Happy to see you again, Petros. A promise is a promise."

He says nothing, but holds her in his arms. After a long while, he releases her and gets her bag from the carousel. When they arrive at his car, Samantha is amazed.

"This is your car?"

"Yeah, it's different from the North American cars, eh?"

He drives slowly along the city streets to show her around and then takes her to his apartment. He tells her that his uncle bought this car for him when he got back from Canada. Samantha has a lot of new things to tell him about Ginno and Vancouver, but she is so eager to be close to him again that in her rush to undress she rips her bra. On the couch she gets on top of him and enjoys his firmness deep inside her with her orgasms coming one after the other.

When the flesh is satisfied, she sits up and looks around in the room. The furniture, the paintings on the walls, the books—all are where they are supposed to be. She lights a cigarette.

"It looks very nice. You furnished it alone?"

"No, Magdalene gave me some help."

She looks into his eyes and says, "Magda is around for good, eh?"

"No, sweetheart, nobody is around for good," he says, avoiding getting into any detail.

The phone rings at this moment, and he gets up to pick it up while she goes to the shower.

"Hello?"

"Hi, how are you?"

It is Magda.

"I'm okay. Samantha arrived today. How are you?"

"Where is she staying, Petros?"

"She is here with me, Magdalene."

Her breath stops for a second.

"Oh, I see. She is there with you right now?"

"Yes, Magda, she is here."

"Then I guess there is no need for me to come to your place, is it?"

He says nothing. Magda doesn't say more either. She knows that she needs to do exactly what her parents have told her to do for the last few days: get away from him.

A strong wind blows southward from the Parnetha Mountain, and the city is engulfed with a cold shroud like an old monk in his penance cell. It is the third of October, and as soon as he gets up in the morning he calls Amalia to let her know that he is not going to school today, and she has to do without him in the lecture room. He has a visitor from Vancouver, Canada, and he intends to take her around the Acropolis grounds and the Agora. Amalia is disappointed to hear this, yet she knows he is the man she would like to be with, even if that comes in short slivers of time here and there.

They are out of the door as soon as Samantha wakes up and finishes her shower. He drives slowly along the busy streets, which are full of buses, cars, taxis, and thousands of motorcycles. He is always amazed how these people on the motorcycles manage to get around the rest of the traffic and still be in one piece. It is something Samantha is amazed about, too. This is something she cannot imagine to see back in Vancouver; it would be madness.

She is very happy that she has him to herself for the day. He parks his car near the Acropolis. They have to hike for a while, so they start the walking right away. She is tired shortly, so Petros slows down and advises her to stop every few minutes to catch her breath. They finally get to the entrance, and she is astonished to see such an eminent monument which has been standing here for over two thousand years.

The wind blew the clouds away, and the sun peeks from the eastern horizon to show the vast blue sky. They walk around in the grounds, and Petros explains to Samantha every detail about the Parthenon, the Karyatides temple, and so on. He tells her the meaning of all the smaller statues engraved on the Metopi of the Parthenon. After that, they saunter to the museum and spend a good hour there admiring the exhibits.

"This is the crown of Athens. Visitors from every place of the world come here. It really makes me proud, Sam."

She looks at him; his eyes are almost full of tears as he says these words, and she smiles at him.

"I know, Petros, I am proud to be here and be with you. I know what it represents in your heart. This is you too; this is part of who you are. I know, my love, truly I do."

This is the first time ever she calls him "my love," and he turns and hugs her in front of all the people in the museum. They walk outside and go toward the edge of the hilltop. Petros shows her the city of Athens below. Samantha is awed by the spectacular view.

"This is really a big city."

"Not only a big city, Sam, but a very old city, too. Don't forget there are records of the first people around here in the eighth century BC. That makes this city twenty-eight centuries old, just imagine that."

Later, they stroll slowly down the steps of the entrance way and make their way to Plaka. They stop at a small tavern to have something to eat. Later they find the Agora building and spend another hour looking around.

The day unfolds slowly, and he enjoys her company wherever he takes her. Then, they get back to the car and he drives toward the

Gulf, where he walked yesterday on his own. On the way there she says, "How is Magda, Petros?"

"She is okay, Sam. Why are you asking?"

"Are you not seeing each other anymore?"

"No, Sam, I don't see anybody that way anymore. I have been involved in so many things that I really don't have the time for any steady relationship, if that's what you mean."

"How are you doing with all your ideas and things you talked to me back in Vancouver? I still believe you may get in trouble with all that. How is the political situation here? Any changes?"

"Nothing yet, Sam, but soon."

"What do you mean by 'soon'? Are you involved in something? Please tell me you are not."

"Samantha, there is a very good chance that the situation will change very soon. You'll see; I believe it is a matter of just weeks, or at the most, months."

"You are involved then, if you know this much. I hope you know how to take care of yourself. You know you are playing with fire."

"Yes, I know, Sam. Don't worry. Nothing is going to happen to me."

They arrive at the waterfront, and he stops the car. He gets out and goes around the car to open the door for her, a gesture he does for the first time, and Samantha enjoys it.

"Let's go down to the sea."

He takes her by the hand and leads the way to the shoreline. Petros notices for the first time that he enjoys the feeling of having her hand in his and smiles at the thought.

"I walked here yesterday before I went to the airport to get you. There is a nice rocky outcrop on the left, let's go over there."

They get to the edge of the land, and she hops from one rock to the other as he sits and looks at her happily. He is really glad seeing her with him. She flew nearly ten thousand kilometers to come and visit him. The vastness of the horizon catches his eyes when she crouches down to the water to get her hands wet.

"Be careful," he yells, but a large wave hits the rock beside her forcefully and splashes up. She is completely wet: her face, her hair, her hands, her clothes, her legs. She gets up and turns over to see the fear on Petros' face. She starts to laugh. She laughs and laughs until he cannot hold himself anymore and does the same.

He runs to the car and brings a towel for her to dry herself.

"Good grief! You are soaking wet." He takes his jacket off and puts it around her shoulders.

"Oh, it's nothing, a lesson for me the most," she answers and feels as happy as ever having him take care of her.

"You'll catch a cold. Let's go home."

"No, no, don't worry; let's stay for a while. It is so nice here."

They take a short walk along the other side of the seashore and she feels a bit better as she gets warmer. She looks at him, wondering how tender and loving he can be. But then she starts to worry about him.

"Petros, have you ever given any thought to the idea of going back to Vancouver?"

"Why would I like to do that?"

"I don't know. This feeling of something bad approaching is in my mind and heart every day. I don't know how to explain it to you. It is just there, and it kills my peace. I can't put it away from my mind."

He tries to calm her down.

"Stop worrying, Sam, I'm a big boy; nothing is going to happen to me."

She takes her cigarettes out and lights one, and then says jokingly, "Come on, have a puff. It isn't going to hurt you."

He does to please her, and after a few coughs, finds that smoking is not really the end of the world. Still, he gives the cigarette back to her with a laugh, "Here you are, Samantha, you just turned me into a smoker. But I don't think I like it," he sits down on a rock, and she stands next to him laughing.

He talks to her for a while about his dreams of making something out of his ideals. Then he finds himself willing to share with Samantha things he hasn't ever shared with Magdalene. He realizes this and looks at her lovingly. He tells her that up to now, he has never been so attracted to a girl.

Samantha is so pleased to hear him say that and asks him to give some thought to the idea of Vancouver, or else she has no other choice but to stay here in Athens with him a lot longer than what she has had in mind.

"You can stay with me as long as you like, Sam," he kisses her.

No sooner do they reach his apartment in the evening than Petros gets a phone call from Antoniou who wants to come over for a while. He agrees, and Antoniou with his friend George Hatzis arrive at his place one hour later.

They talk for a while about the upcoming demonstration when Antoniou tells Petros that he is in regular contact with the youth organization of the polytechnic school, and they have started planning an action that calls for a large disobedience drive within the grounds of the school. Petros is happy to hear that, and he signs a petition form when they hand it to him. Petros hugs Sam when the two students leave. He knows that she is worried. He kisses her lips. They undress and hop in the shower together. They make passionate love and later on lie on the sofa enjoying a cigarette together.

The door bell rings.

Samantha gets up and presses the speaker button. Magda's voice is heard: "Hello is Petros in?"

"Yes, he is here. Magda, is it you?"

"Yes, Samantha, I'd like to come up."

Sam turns to Petros who nods and she presses the button. She goes back to the bathroom to give Petros and Magda some privacy. In a minute Magda arrives. She hugs Petros with tears in her eyes.

"You must go. Leave, as fast as you can. Take Samantha and go."

He is astonished.

"What are you talking about, Magdalene?"

"Petros, they are coming for you. A man approached my father and told him everything. They are coming for you, one of these days, perhaps in a couple of days. My dad asked me to stay away from you back in September, after our evening at the dean's place.

That man, Alvarezos, he is of no good. He is perhaps the instrument for all this."

Samantha comes out of the bathroom at this moment, thinking it would be best to say hello to Magda, but is shocked to see the expression on her face.

"What is it, Magda?"

"I am fine, Samantha. Good to see you," Magda prefers to say nothing to her about Petros' trouble. She turns and looks at Petros' eyes, begging him to do as she has asked him to do.

"I have to go. I'll call you, okay?"

"Okay, Magdalene thanks for the news. I'll talk to you later."

Magda leaves. Petros paces around the room, not knowing what to say to Samantha, who is totally puzzled. Magda's family is well connected to the circles of Athens, so what she says is not just theories.

"What did Magda tell you, Petros?" Sam can't hold back anymore.

"She is worried about something, Sam, same as you are worried. Women always worry about things."

Samantha doesn't like the sound of it, yet she knows Petros Spathis, and he is not in any mood to reveal to her what just happened. Tomorrow perhaps she will dig it out of him in a different way. Women, she thinks, always have a way of getting something out of a man when he least expects it.

10

The next day he has to go to school. Samantha agrees to go to the center of the city to see the sites and do some shopping. They decide that they will meet again at his school in the afternoon and spend the rest of the day together.

When he arrives at the university, Amalia is in his office. They have a coffee together and prepare for the day's lecture. Amalia has an outline of the subject, taxation.

The lecture goes very well, and at the end, Amalia and he come back to his office where they work on tomorrow's class. He calls the cafeteria and orders a couple of sandwiches for both of them, and when the food is delivered, they eat and discuss at the same time, although her mind is more than the work at hand. She moves closer and kisses him. He is caught by surprise and does not want to disappoint her. He locks his door. They are on the couch, and he is on top of her in a matter of seconds. She responds passionately, and he loves seeing that she reaches her climax even before he has a chance to do the same. However, she has a different pleasure for him: she takes his firmness in her mouth and within a few movements he does as he did the day before, right there in her mouth. She has no problem this time and stays with him for a few seconds more until he relaxes completely. She then runs to the washroom to clean up, followed by him. There, as she lathers him, he turns her around against the vanity cabinet where she leans, and he is behind her. He drives her wild as he pushes himself deep inside her. Amalia is in heaven. However, before they get to the point of no return, the phone rings, and Petros gets dressed quickly and answers the phone.

Antoniou is on the line: "Petros, go, leave right now. Go. They are coming for you. Go."

He is flabbergasted. He doesn't know what to say or do. He says to Amalia, "Something is about to happen. You've got to go."

"What is it?" she asks and quickly puts her skirt on.

"I don't know yet, Antoniou just warned me of something imminent. Get ready and go." He unlocks the door for her.

But the door is pushed open, and two men are there with Alvarezos.

They grab him. They put cuffs on him. They hold his arm and without even letting him get his jacket, they take him away.

Amalia is left there speechless. She sits down shaking, and her mind visualizes a million bad things when she realizes what just happened in front of her eyes. She gets up and runs to the hallway toward a classroom; perhaps she can find Antoniou. He is indeed there.

"They took him."

"I know. I saw the trustee and the plainclothes."

"God, what can we do now?" Amalia wonders aloud.

"I have a few things I need to do, yet we have to stick around and see whether Samantha is coming over here to meet him. He doesn't have any other scheduled classes, which means he has already made arrangements for her to meet him somewhere. Let's hope that that place is here, otherwise we can hope to find her later tonight at his apartment. Stay here and keep your eyes open to see if she comes. I'll run and get the news to a couple of other guys."

She nods, and he goes away, leaving her in the middle of the hallway with all these students going about their normal business. Amalia suddenly feels extremely lonely. She goes back to his office and tries to grasp why they would take him away like that, without anybody saying anything to him. The government trustee, what is his role in all of this? Is this real? Does this happen every day in Athens? She can't find any answer. Half an hour later, which is three in the afternoon, Antoniou gets to the school and finds Amalia still in Petros' office.

"I couldn't find Samantha. It's best that we don't hang around here. Let's go."

They leave and Antoniou spots Samantha by the front gates of the school.

"Samantha," they both run to her.

Antoniou tells her what happened and Samantha's mouth drops open.

He knows what she is thinking,

"I don't know where they took him, or what they are going to do to him, but you need to leave, Samantha. Go to the Canadian embassy, and try to go back home, the sooner the better. You should be safe, after all, you are a Canadian citizen; yet you don't know how far these pigs can go."

"I can't leave now. I have to stay and help him."

"Samantha, this is our war, not yours. This is our battle, and we will fight it to the end. Trust me: he'll not stay forever wherever they take him. You have my word on this. But you need to look after yourself first. That is something he would like you to do. Just go; leave this place. When are you due to leave?"

"My ticket is for seven days from now, but I was thinking of staying with him a bit longer, perhaps a month or so. He asked me to stay." She turns to Amalia, but Amalia looks the other way.

Antoniou thinks quickly and tells Samantha, "Go to the embassy, talk to someone, and see whether anything can come out of it. You never know; sometimes help comes from the most unexpected places. We'll keep in touch. Are you going to stay in his apartment until you leave?"

"I think so. Call me there later. First, I'll go to the embassy."

They go their separate ways. Samantha runs to the street, flags a taxi down, and gives the driver the address of the embassy, which is about fifteen minutes away. When arriving, she rushes to the office and demands to see the ambassador. The clerk doesn't take her seriously; Samantha becomes so desperate that she starts a raucous cry in the hallway. The clerk takes her by the arm, "What is it, Miss? What is your name? Let me see your passport."

She searches in her purse frantically to find her passport, "I'm sorry, but it is a life and death situation. I need to see the ambassador, please, please."

The clerk looks at her passport and tries to cool her down, "Okay, Samantha, what is it you need to talk to the ambassador? Whose life is in danger?"

She tries to explain to the man everything; he can't follow her and interrupts, "I don't think we can do anything for this man, but let me call the ambassador's council and see whether he can see you without appointment."

Two minutes later she is in the office of Peter Clark, the ambassador's councilor, who asks her to sit down. She repeats the story about Petros Spathis and his abduction from the grounds of the University of Athens.

Peter Clark shakes his head, saying, "There is nothing we can do, Samantha. He is a Greek citizen and this is a matter of their police or whatever security system they have. It has nothing to do with us. We cannot interfere with Greece's internal affairs. What is this man to you anyway?"

"I love him."

"How did you meet him?"

She told him that they met in Vancouver when he did his MBA at the University of British Columbia.

He stops and looks deep into Samantha's eyes: "Even if he isn't a Canadian citizen, we may be able to treat him as one of our future citizens since he is married to you. But you are not married, are you?"

Samantha's mind sees a thread of hope in his words and lies flatly on his face.

"Yes, we got married before he left. That's why I'm here, visiting my husband."

Peter Clark smiles a broad smile.

"Well, Samantha, we need to see proper documentation to verify your marriage. Then the ambassador may be able to call a few people. Do you have these papers with you?"

"No, but I'll call my father and see when I can have them mailed to me."

"Alright then, you know what you have to do. Without these papers I'm afraid none of us in this embassy will be able to talk to anyone regarding the future of this man."

As soon as she reaches Petros' apartment, she gets on the phone waking her father up, since it is seven o'clock in the morning back in Vancouver. He is surprised to hear her voice. She explains to him what she needs him to do.

"Sam, sweetheart, how can I go about and do this?"

"Dad, I have never asked you for anything serious before; this is what I want you to do. Please, you are the only hope Petros and I have. Please, do it for me."

Ginno takes a deep breath.

"Okay, I'll try my best."

"Thank you, Daddy, I love you. Please do this right away and phone me here as soon as you have it. Please send me some money, too; I don't think I have enough, okay?"

11

Each stone is placed in position by the hand of the craftsman one on top of another to form the impenetrable totality. Only the door is cracked and warped from age and careless use. There are many dates carved on it. One is 27-7-1939—the beginning of someone's new life, someone's new experience. It is the combination of insanity and frenzy, of logic and wisdom that characterizes the soul of those who must live within these walls. Here, a dance takes place sometimes by death, sometimes with the person's fates, or other times with April and its wildflowers. Here, one finds misfortune with its set boundaries and a strange sweetness that offers nothing, but gives the Nirvana of the soul with a plain numbness. Scared and closed within, indifferent and furious at the same time—just like the immature joy of a first erotic union of young flesh with the fresh carelessness which a seventeen-year-old may have.

That strange shudder goes through his body again, the same as all other times when something bad is about to happen. So it has come so near, this desired and cursed tragic hour? He shivers again.

He hears footsteps in the corridor, the familiar footsteps of the guard: it is time of reveille. So it is morning already then. This day, today, is going to bring everything or nothing, like all other days he has spent in this devout prison cell. This morning will separate logic from insanity once and for all, or it is going to further tangle all the threads with which fate spins her web. He is like a marionette in the hands of a master who suddenly decides to stop the show. All movement ceases, and the wind refuses to hear the cry of a man, of a man's heart, or better yet, the cry of a man's dream.

The guard leaves. Petros gets up and takes the familiar three and a half steps to the door. For a second he feels as though some magic power is going to open the door wide and allow him to run, to escape. But then he realizes the bitter game that his imagination plays on him and the tragedy of his life. Having nothing else to do, he starts pacing from one side of the cell to the other horizontally, perpendicularly, and diagonally without stepping off the borders of one flat stone on the floor; he is able to do this even with his eyes closed. He sits at the edge of his bed and lights a cigarette, his new habit. Was it in here that he started this habit? He cannot remember, and then his mind travels to Samantha. Yes, it was with her when he tried it for the first time last month; has he been here for a month or for a century?

He takes two deep puffs and coughs. Within these walls, time becomes slippery like an old man's memory. He tries to recall what he doesn't like to remember . . . They came right into his office and took him away in front of the eyes of Amalia, who stared with wide open eyes and a choked breath as she witnessed the abduction. His memory is preserved, untouched by time, but his eyes are beginning to weaken. When night falls, the world around him, the walls of his cell, the door, the ceiling, even the stars which are visible through the iron barred window become blurry, difficult to discern. This seems to prove that the irrevocable, redeeming hour is approaching. He sits up on his bed as the thought of Samantha comes to him: what happened to her after he got picked up? Does she know what happened to him? Did anybody tell her? Does anybody really know where he is?

His eyes focus on the door, seeing it as if for the first time, and this brings him back to reality. He takes another puff of his cigarette. He taps it and watches the ashes fall until they reach the stone floor. He steps on the ashes and then blows them away, a monotonous, routine action. Has he become a robot? A strong silent cry, desperate, frightened, comes from the depths of his soul . . . I am a Human . . . Am I? He tests himself by counting or doing simple arithmetic calculations. He is still able to do them; then, he is able to organize things. What can he organize from a prison? What about Samantha? What happened to Amalia? He is sorry that he has drawn them into this predicament, and senses that Magda will be protected by the wealth and power of her family.

Questions and questions and he cannot find any answers. He doesn't even know what is going to happen to him. How long is he going to be in prison? Is there anything anybody can do for him? Always the same thoughts and the same questions before he falls asleep and finds himself in the same familiar place, not able to distinguish whether he is alive or already dead; whether he walks like a man or flies like a bird. Who is that old man with white hair whom he meets quite often in his half awake and half asleep state? Whose white dog is that with the red eyes and the ever hungry fangs? Is he hallucinating or is he sane as any other man?

His cigarette burns to the end, hurting his finger before he throws it away. He shivers from the pain. He feels the need to yell at someone, to send everyone to hell, all of them. But he remains silent and lies on the bed still, and then again comes this strange ominous shuddering. His whole body tingles. He scratches it, again and again with fury, trying to feel pain rather than this ferocious itchy shudder which is nothing else but a presentiment. Is the hour so near?

He goes to the basin and rinses his face with a little water. He feels as though he could see himself in an imaginary mirror. His hollow eyes are colorless and expressionless; his lips no longer look attractive as they did when Samantha pressed her love on them; his hair is disheveled, thin, uncombed, and dirty. He tries to comb it with his fingers as if to make him look better.

Can he make them understand that he has done nothing wrong, and he deserves to be treated better? One way or another he has already won his first battle. He is the first opposing voice against them. He has planted the seed in a barren field. He has to do it although he didn't expect this result: jail. Righteousness and logic cannot compete with their established system, no matter how clear and correct his voice is. But things can change. It is his bravo. It is the beginning.

He opens his diary. He sees the pages filled with pure, clear truth, one line after another. Turning to a new page, he takes a pencil and writes today's entry. A hesitant hand, a hesitant mind, a hesitant pencil... He begins: "My essence feels that deliverance is nearer. I have decided to escape. Truly who wouldn't think of this when in a cell? But I have to first find the way. I'd like to imagine that I have already found the way, and I am a free man. I imagine that I have already escaped. I am free. Free? Is it possible under today's conditions?"

He stops writing. The questions soar round and round in his head like a tornado of vultures. He moves, but for all human purposes he is quite dead. He has to get out. Period. Wrung by the fatigue manufactured by the deep and prolonged depression, he allows his body to collapse back into the filthy pillow which stinks from all the previous prisoners' perspiration and tears.

His eyes stop on the outline of the door once more: it is open! He jumps up and runs to it, but as quickly he pulls back. He covers his face with both hands: "My God, how can it be? What lion-like strength do I have to have in order to stay sane?"

His mind is barren now; it cannot come up with anything useful or show him what he wants. The only thing he knows is that he is very tired of all this. The emptiness of the prison routine takes life out of him and does not allow him to find himself as he always had when he was ready for the battle, ready for any battle. God, let it come then: he wants to be remembered by his friends and the people whom he never betrayed. He starts to wonder again: How long has he been imprisoned? What happened to the plans he made with Antoniou and the others? Did they carry through with the civil disobedience? What happened to those other students? Have they been arrested as well? What happened to Samantha?

Questions, questions. No answers.

His eyes become heavy and he sees himself running in the middle of a wheat field in the harvest season. He runs and runs and finally reaches the end of the yellow field. There it is a small murmuring creek with refreshing water. He bends down to get a drink, he is extremely thirsty. But how strange: whenever he stretches his neck to reach the flowing water—he can see it, that is certain—recedes before he can get any, no matter how hard he tries. Tantalizing, tantalizing . . . he suddenly wakes up and realizes that he is the cursed Tantalus, who is doomed to be tortured. He is so thirsty.

"I am not cursed," he starts to convince himself. "If I can endure this, all the rest will be so simple and fall into place just as the stones of the mosaic fit together."

The usual knock on the door takes him away from his thoughts, and he walks over to get his meal when the guard opens the door half way. The duty he has toward his struggle tells him that he has to eat his food and stay healthy the best he can. No matter what he is fed, he eats.

After the food, he lights a cigarette and lies in bed again. The thoughts which never leave him for a minute are here again, as always. His past life begins to unfold in front of him like the petals of a beautiful flower. All its fragrance, all its color, all its glory—he can smell them; he can. It is time that all these join together to take flesh and bones, enough so that someday, someone will be able to see them as a whole, to see them worthy of excellence.

So he sits up with his legs crossed and writes on his diary. The wind blows outside, and he can hear the sound which penetrates the glass of his window and gives him the sense of being alive. He feels cold, especially his left foot. He looks down and notices a hole on the sock, and two of his toes poke out of it. He gets up and finds a little box from his drawer. He opens it and takes out a needle and thread. He passes the thread through the eye as if he has done this all his life: he is not bad with this at all. He mends his sock, puts it on again, and then throws the little box back. He climbs back on the bed and covers his legs with the edge of the blanket.

This October day is quite frosty. His hands and feet are still frozen, so his efforts to continue writing are in vain. All he can do is lie in bed and cover completely. He lights another cigarette, his mind running to Samantha. She started him with this smoking thing the day he took her to the beach. What a fun day it was. A faint smile suffuses all his face; he finds warmth in his heart again.

He then gets an urge to see the outside, so he wraps himself with the blanket and walks to the small window. It is too tall; he pulls his bed under the window and climbs on the headboard. From here he can see the courtyard. The wind has subsided; small raindrops whirl in the light wind. It is as though they were dancing for him. He stands there, mesmerized by the rain. Ever since he was a child, he has liked to stay still at someplace and watch the rain fall.

Soon the wind is completely gone, yet the rain keeps on dancing down to the ground. Slowly the courtyard becomes wetter and wetter, and the fountain in the opposite corner begins to glow. The stones of the courtyard are also shining, and the brightness of the evening reminds him of the luminous moon of last night.

A strange sensation squeezes his heart: he wants to cry, to yell to scream as loud as he can.

It is then he hears some strange noise from the next cell, number 321. The prisoner has been making these noises for quite a while. It sounds like the prisoner is tapping a dish against the wall. Is he trying to communicate with him? He suddenly asks himself. Yes, there is a certain rhythm in them: da-daaa-daaa, da-da-da, daaa-daaa-daaa... The Morse code. Yes, yes, of course. He curses himself for not having paid attention to these signals before. He brings his ear closer to the wall.

"Who are you?" is the code.

He is thankful he remembers the code.

"I am Petros," he quickly knocks back with his dish.

"And what else?"

"Petros Spathis."

"Thanks for answering me."

"Why you are here?"

"I don't know."

"You don't know?"

"No, not really." Petros signals.

"It's too late now, we will talk more tomorrow."

All is quiet again.

Why hadn't he noticed the meaning of the tapping for such a long time? All this time he just thought the neighbor was a strange fellow. Petros gets up, feeling truly happy for the first time. There is someone who wants to find out about him. Now he may be able to talk to someone here and there. He goes to the other wall, takes his dish and starts knocking on it rhythmically but gets no answer. He concludes that perhaps the prisoner is no longer in the cell.

He pushes his bed back where it belongs and lies down under the blanket, bundling himself to warm up. He also covers his head so he can warm up himself faster with his breath. He makes a small opening to breathe exactly the way he used to when he was a young boy during winters in the village. After a while, his legs start hurting because of being curled up. He is warm enough now, so he stretches his legs and soon falls asleep.

Eight days have gone by since Samantha talked to her dad. Then he calls her to tell her that he has gotten everything she needs and is to courier the package to her today. It is morning in Vancouver, the morning of October the sixteenth. She is happy and gets her purse to go out for breakfast. Before she leaves, the phone rings again and it is Magda this time. She wants to come and see Samantha.

Half an hour later, Magdalene rings the doorbell and Sam lets her in.

"Samantha, I don't know how close you and Petros are, but I have to let you know. You may be in extreme danger. The people who are after him are very powerful and they may come for you also . . ."

Samantha interrupts her with a smile, "Thank you, Magda, for taking the time and for caring enough to come here and warn me, but I'm not afraid of anything. Nobody can touch me, I'm a Canadian citizen. Who is there to harm me anyway?"

Obviously Sam doesn't understand what it means to be under military rule. Magdalene feels that she has to clear a few things for her.

"Sam, this is not Canada; this is not a democratically governed country. These people will stop at nothing to stay in power. They don't care whether you are a Canadian citizen or a citizen of any other country for that matter. They imprison many many people who are in their way. You think they care about where you come from?"

"I'm not going anywhere. Petros and I got married back in Vancouver, and when I get my papers from my dad the next few days, I'll have him freed."

Magda is stunned with such a revelation. It can't be true. Petros wouldn't lie to her about something like this.

"No, all this is in your mind, isn't it, Sam?" she begs, tears in her eyes.

Sam knows what she has to do, tell her the truth: "It is the only way the Canadian Embassy may get involved and get him out of prison, which means if this happens, he has to leave the country with me."

Magda's mind works quickly. "Good move, Sam. I suppose the necessary documents are properly executed?"

"My father knows a lot of people, Magda."

"Good. You can count on me also. If you need a witness, you can say I was present at your wedding in Vancouver when I was there, okay?"

Samantha smiles and hugs her, hoping that they will work together to get Petros freed.

Magda leaves.

Three days later Samantha receives her marriage papers from the courier company. She goes to the embassy right away and finds the clerk, Peter Clark. She stares at his eyes as he peruses the documents.

"Well, Samantha. I'll give these to the ambassador and ask him to intervene. But be patient."

"I know. Can you please see that I get to visit him?"

"Well I don't know about that. I'll do some inquiries. I suggest you leave his apartment and find a hotel room for yourself. They may go and look in his apartment for whatever and you shouldn't be there when that happens."

"No, on the contrary, I'm determined to stay at my husband's place; who is going to bother me?"

Peter chooses to say nothing else. Samantha leaves him, feeling optimistic.

The next morning, Petros is awakened by the knock on his door. It is the guard making his morning rounds. He hears the guard cough and sneeze. "Ha, he caught a cold," Petros thinks, but he feels too chilly to move his facial muscles. He jumps up, gets washed, and begins to do his morning exercise routine beginning with stomping his feet. He exercises often in his cell to keep his body fit. By any means, he works to retain his vigor in this cursed rat hole. Other times, when he is cold and depressed and too lazy to exercise, he takes a pencil and tries to draw something high on the wall; the higher he reaches, the warmer he gets as he exerts himself to stretch upward, and eventually feels the sweat running down his arms.

He hears the guard's steps in the corridor. It is time for their morning meal. Petros hears the cell doors down the hall open one by one to pass the prisoners their ration of tea, bread, and olives. Occasionally, two or three familiar phrases are exchanged between some prisoners and the guard.

Petros takes his tea, and stares at it. Then he tries to take a sip. It is the same taste in his mouth, every morning, and the same revolting smell of tea boiled in a big cauldron that they probably use for a lot of purposes. He goes back to his bed, sits, and dips his bread in the tea, stirring it and leaving it for a moment or two to soften the bread, as always. Then he bites it, sixteen bites in all to eat the bread as he has counted, and finishes it with eight olives. He is sure that without the taste of the olive in his mouth, he will not ever be able to finish the tea.

He eats as slowly as he did when he was young. His stomach growls satisfactorily, and he feels a bit better. Getting up, he goes to the basin and washes his dish and spoon. Returning to his bed, he lights a cigarette. His cigarette package is now empty, so he throws it into the garbage.

He lies there, drawn into his thoughts again. He is put away because the junta does not want to bother trying to understand that Greece needs a democratic government working for the people. They just want to shut his message off rather than giving it a chance to see the light of day. They cannot afford to have him walking around freely and spreading his words to the populace who could take up arms and destroy the phony world the junta has built to fool the people. He is the man with the new ideas, and new ideas mean the old ones are not good anymore. All new ideas are bad for the junta; only the black book and the army regulations are what they can count on.

The question is how long they can keep the Greek populace under their powerful fist?

No matter what, their days are counted. His day of liberation may come sooner than he thinks. When Petros is free, they'll see what his new ideas will mean to the public. "Yes, Petros Spathis, you have done what you are destined to do; you have spoken for them," he says aloud to hear his own words, making sure the walls of the cell do as well. "Yes, you have spoken; yet who has listened to you?"

"Did the wind listen and turn its auspicious fan your way? Did the sun listen and light your steps? Did the rain listen and fertilize all thirsty wheat fields? Did your fellow citizens listen and start your eternal revolution? Who listened to you, Petros Spathis?" An echo from the breeze in the courtyard seems to ask the same questions.

"Even if one reed in the dry riverbed heard of your song, it's worthy of your life. Even if one little chickadee heard of your love, it is well worthy of your death. Even if only a little worm heard of your war against the corrupted government, it is worthy of your dream. Nothing of what you have done is wasted, Petros Spathis. Nothing of what you have said is in vain. Nothing of what you have sung is lost in this war. Rejoice, Petros Spathis, your deed, your song, and your war are all well worthy of your stature," the echo continues.

Stupid pride, he thinks. A single tear slides down his left cheek.

12

This is the first time they take him out. He follows the guards, not knowing where he is going. As they go by cell 321 he wonders for an instance whether he wants to say something to the prisoner in there he only knows as 321; a farewell perhaps, or encouragement to keep him going. 321 must have glued his eyes on the keyhole to watch Petros walk by. Petros slows his pace to try and make eye contact but the guard behind him pushes him on, and he obeys. They get to the end of the dark hallway and start a descent in a stairwell which lasts for a quite a while. He counts that they step about thirty steps lower. When they get to the level he notices a very dark, narrow corridor. He starts to think that he is to meet his destiny in this place where no other human beings exist except for the two guards, and Petros Spathis in between.

    He clearly hears the sewage water running underground, beneath the floors. He feels his death is waiting for him at the end of this corridor. However, they come to the end and turn to continue another long walk down a corridor, and then they get to a stairway. The guards force him to walk up; it is twenty-three steps. At the last step another corridor begins. Now he can see some light coming through from the odd opening above. They force him to walk faster now. They stop in front of a door, and the first guard bangs twice with his fist. Footsteps approach the door, and a key turns the lock. The door opens, and the guards push Petros into a large room, empty except for a small desk and two chairs. He is seated under the light. In one corner a stove is lit, and the room is warm. The two guards salute the man, who must be a captain, then leave the room, and the man who opened the door sits on the desk. He seems familiar, but Petros cannot see him clearly; the light above him is blinding his eyes. Another door to his right opens, one he had not noticed earlier, and another guard enters, stands at attention, salutes the captain, and moves off to a corner of the room where he will remain standing. The officer opens a file and begins to flip through it, stopping once in a while to read something. He then invites Petros to move his chair closer, which Petros does, and asks Petros if he wants a cigarette. Petros takes one, the man takes another one for himself, and they both light up. Petros tries to see his features, suddenly the captain says, "Well, 322, what do you think of your new home?"

He gets caught off-guard by being called 322—in jail there is no names, just numbers; each person has a number, with its own pain written on its face.

"It's like jail," he replies coldly.

"But of course. You are in jail, Professor." The captain takes a long puff from his cigarette and slowly blows the smoke upward.

"Tell me exactly what happened on the ninth of September in your class. What subject did you discuss that day?"

Petros tries hard to remember what he talked about to the students that day—and lo and behold, yes, it was the subject of business management for medium-sized companies. Why would they want to know? But he leaves the question behind and starts to explain. However, as he does that, the captain interrupts.

"How many students were in attendance that day?"

"I don't remember the exact number; usually we have about fifty to sixty people in class. What difference does it make anyway?"

"You are not the one who asks questions here, Spathis. I am. You are to give me answers, nothing else. Tell me, Spathis, you think your views and theories are more effective, right?"

"Yes, they can be much more effective, when implemented."

"You think they will improve the lives of the people dramatically?"

"Definitely, when implemented."

"Well, what stops you from proposing them to the faculty or the ministry?"

"The faculty and the ministry don't care about what I believe."

"Aha, that is why you conspired to overthrow this government?" the captain says coldly.

Petros is totally aghast.

"I didn't conspire against anybody. I don't agree with the methods of the junta, but I didn't conspire anything..."

"The 'junta,' Professor? Is that what you call our government? This is the best revolution this country has ever seen, but you call it a junta?"

"What is it then? Duly elected by the people?"

"I question, Spathis, and you only give me answers," the captain repeats.

They continue. As the subject changes from time to time the captain will stop Petros and throw in a stupid comment like: "How many cigarettes do you smoke a day Professor?"

Then the interrogation begins again with its formal air, and Petros answers whatever question the captain proposes. Again and again he has to say things he already said earlier.

Then the captain asks, "Who is this Antoniou student, Spathis?"

Petros stares toward captain who is still indistinguishable from of the glaring light, and tries to figure out the reason for such question.

"He is one of the brightest students I have."

"Are you a communist, Professor?"

"No, I am certainly not..."

"Yet, all these ideas of yours are nothing else but communism, simple and straight."

"I only care for the well being of my countrymen, particularly the ones who are jailed without a trial, the unfortunate ones who have their own beliefs."

"You mean the ones like you, Professor?"

"Yes, all the people who are in jail for political reasons. These are Greek citizens like everyone else. They have the rights of a free citizen."

"But, they are all communists, Professor . . ."
"No, they are not."
"What is the size of your shoes?"
Petros stays silent for a moment.
"Forty-two . . ."

The captain looks at his file; then turns the interrogation to a heated monologue about communism and the perils of such a system. Petros Spathis listens quietly, which frustrates the captain because he is discovering that he cannot find any worthy charges against this man who has been described to him as a formidable enemy, an enemy of the country. Petros notices the captain's expression, the same exasperation a hunter has when he sees his trap empty, without game.

The captain takes his cigarettes out again and offers one to Petros who says no, thank you. The captain observes Petros sharply and gets up. He walks to the door, and then, as if changing his mind, goes to his guard who has been standing in the corner silently, and whispers something in his ear. Then without saying anything to Petros, the captain leaves the room. The guard walks over and sits at the desk with the prisoner. Petros also finds the guard familiar but cannot pinpoint who he is. "Now you are in trouble," the guard says suddenly. "This other man who is to come is sly like a fox. Watch out; if you want to come out of this prison alive you'd better told him all you know."

He leans a bit closer. He has blue eyes that glow under the lamp's light, thin lips, a heavy nose, and a large chin. Now Petros is sure he knows him from somewhere. He wants to ask him about that, but the door opens again, and another captain enters.

The guard stands up and salutes him, then goes back to his corner. The captain, after scolding the guard for speaking with Petros, sits and smiles at the professor.

"Tell me, prisoner, what was the subject of your lecture on Thursday, the seventeenth of September?"

Petros looks at the man and tries to recollect the subject of discussion that day. Yes, he analyzed the taxation system and how it affects most people. He tells the captain all he remembers, but the man doesn't seem to be happy with what he has heard. He takes out a document from his file and studies it. For an instant their eyes meet. Their strengths are measured in a flash, and the scale tips on Petros' side.

"Can I ask something, Captain?"

"What is it, prisoner?"

"How is my family?"

"Your family is just fine, 322."

"How long am I to be here?"

"That depends on you, prisoner. If you tell us what we want to know, you may go home soon."

The questioner gets up and begins pacing around the room. Petros stretches his legs to get rid of the numbness. The captain approaches the guard and whispers something in his ear. The guard leaves the room. They are alone now. He approaches Petros and leans against the desk, starting to talk about general things, things which are not relevant to what he is here for. Petros listens to all this carefully—there is no alternative—although he desperately needs to lie down to rest.

"Take your chair, prisoner, and come and sit here," the captain motions him to one of the corners.

Petros obeys, and when he is sitting alone in the designated place, the captain leaves him alone and goes behind the door only to come back one minute later and yell, "Come here, prisoner, take your chair and come closer. Who told you to sit there?"

Petros pulls his chair into the middle of the room and sits again under the light without any comment.

The guard comes back, says something to the captain in a low tone, and goes back to his post by the corner. The captain starts pacing again, circling Petros. He then goes back to the desk and makes notes. Finally, the captain replaces all the documents in the file and gets up to leave. Petros looks at him, waiting for him to say something. The captain gives him an indifferent look, "Goodbye, 322, I will see you again soon."

Petros Spathis goes to bed early this night right after the evening distribution of food. He eats his spaghetti with no appetite. Then he tries to write an entry in his diary but is unable to come up with something worth writing. The only thing which never leaves him is his thoughts. They come at any time to weaken his mind. He wants them, he asks for them to keep him company; but most of the times he can't bear them. They torture him at times. Other times, they seek revenge or resolve to an absolution. Normally, he does things after a good discussion with himself. But now his thoughts come as uninvited Furies to disturb his solitude, to remind him that he is in this cursed cell.

He tries to take philosophically the injustice of his position, but all he can think of is these menacing boundaries of the web they have woven him into. He turns to the south, and a violent storm hits him right on the face; he turns to the north, and the enraged wind lifts him high up and throws him into the rugged rocks; he turns to the east, and the burning morning sun blinds his eyes; and he turns to the west, and the pain of the forthcoming end and the injustice of it all destroys him. He is trapped, and around him the masses move and live at the commands of the dictators.

They tried to fool him in the interrogation; he saw the irony on their faces; he heard their cunning laughter, and his blood went to his head, burning him. Yet, although choking out of frustration, he managed to stay afloat. He chokes again, feeling a strange power tightening around his throat; his breath is cut. He shivers.

Then all of a sudden he is not in the middle of the agora with the masses around him. There is no mockery; there is no cunning laughter. He is somewhere else: it is Sunday morning; he is in church, his heart has opened up, and innocent smiling faces greet him. It is like those unforgettable days when his students gathered around him, listening to him, assimilating everything he said. He was among them, he lived as they did, he listened to what they told him, he made efforts to understand them, and they appreciated him.

Suddenly, the letter he read once in the monastery in Crete comes back to his memory. It is as if the handwritten words have taken on flesh and bones and are dancing around like the phantoms of all the dead poets:

> ... Occasionally, brother, the opportunity is given to us to do something in the service of improving the collective, by whom we measure our own human meaning. We were seduced by the promises of the mainland government into believing that, with their assistance, there was a possibility of effective action. The promises, of course, were only the carrot. And we were the goat—so eager to reach the vegetable, we forgot we were pulling a heavy cart whose contents would benefit the mainland at the expense of the island. When it was over, it was clear enough: nothing had been achieved and almost everything had been lost. A foiled revolution leaves circumstances even more squalid than those of the status quo against which the revolution was perpetrated. That we would have succeeded against the Turks with the promised backing of the mainland is certain. We have lost, but we also have learned. I shall always believe we could have won, and I shall never forgive the mainland of the ruin visited upon us through trusting them...

How long has he been like this lost in his thoughts? How long has he been sitting like this on his bed, still, with the company of his thoughts? He gets up and starts pacing... *Tak! Tak!* His shoes play with the floor. His mind goes to the students:

"Why one should be obliged to enlist in the army, Professor?"

Petros' answer comes clear as a bell: "Truly. Why should they?"

The student was disappointed; he had expected Professor Spathis to be more aggressive and innovative. He had expected him to sanction nobody, burn the whole world, and build a new one on its place. Yet Petros was ambivalent at that time, and now when he remembers this, he feels so regretful.

What are the noises? He stops his pacing and pulls his bed under the window. He climbs on top of the headboard. The wing across from him is in flames; fire and smoke comes out of all windows. Someone has started a fire.

The guards are running up and down in the courtyard, confused as much by the fire as by the orders the commander is yelling at them. He is a fat man with a big belly; he is only wearing pajamas and slippers. Frantically shouting and motioning, he tries with all his might to direct those under him. The guards are half awake, half dressed, and their boots untied. Someone brings a ladder and leans it against the wall beneath a window but immediately realizes it is impossible to get inside with the fire and the iron bars in their way. A group of guards with blankets in their hands try to enter the wing through one door, but the smoke and flames are so strong that give up after a couple of minutes. Petros watches everything closely from his perch. One guard is now saying something to the commander and pointing to the wing where Petros' cell is located.

Two minutes barely go by when hurried footsteps sound in the corridor. They are opening the cell doors. "Everyone out, quickly, take your blanket and come out."

Petros is already dressed. He picks up his blanket and follows the guards out. They run into the yard. The commander is waiting expectantly for them.

"Hurry, hurry, guards and prisoners, go over there. Do whatever you can, we must put the fire out quickly," he points and shouts.

The commander splits them into two groups, and Petros belongs to the one who have to run inside with the blankets. The other one find some small buckets and other kinds of containers to bring water and throw it through the cell window. Inside the building, the prisoners choke from the smoke and the heat. Petros beats the flames with his blanket like the others. Little by little they succeed in isolating the fire. At one point he stops to stretch his aching back, and his glance accidentally falls onto the window where he sees a man looking at him as if he's been waiting for Petros to notice him for a long time. The man motions to Petros to talk to him. Is he 321? Petros slowly approaches the window where the other man is.

"With the dish at the wall," the other man tells him in a low tone and disappears.

Petros understands very well what he means, but was puzzled by the man's secretive manner.

Slowly the fire is put out and they find a shapeless burned mass in the corner of a cell. It must be the prisoner who started the fire. The revolting smell of his body is spread all over the area.

The guards stand there, looking at him without saying anything. Someone hides his face with his hands.

Petros approaches the corpse, bends down, and covers him with a blanket.

"Farewell, rest in peace," he whispers, then addresses the prisoners and guards, "one more human being is dead; may he rest in peace."

A guard looks at him angrily. What the hell does he mean? Three other prisoners make the sign of the cross.

The commander appears at the cell door.

"Bravo fellows. We did very well."

But then he sees the corpse covered by the blanket, and he goes crazy, yelling at the dead body: "Pig! Scum! You wanted to burn all of us like rats."

One of the prisoners jumps forward threateningly, but two others held him back.

"Easy, George, easy."

The commander realizes his mistake and stands still for a moment. Then on his way out of the cell, he utters, "May he rest in peace."

His head is bowed to avoid the glances of the prisoners. A guard with the badge on his sleeve orders, "All prisoners go to the yard. Two of you, go and get this body."

Petros steps forward, trying to grab the charred corpse when the man who spoke to him earlier stops him.

"Not you," he whispers.

Everybody starts to move, following the two prisoners with the body. They put him down where the guard points and return to the group. Petros quickly glances around; there must be about twenty prisoners. The commander arrives at this moment. He is now dressed in his uniform as though he were starting off to war. He speaks in a meek voice: "As you all saw, we had an accident. One of your fellow prisoners, may he rest in peace, started a fire. You understand well that he was not in his right mind."

The commander stops for a moment and then continues,

"Fortunately, it didn't spread to a lot of cells, and we managed to control it." He says the words, "we managed" with extreme pride and acts as though he, too, worked hard to beat the fire with his blanket. "I want to congratulate you all for your effort. You and the guards prove that when a common enemy appears, you will all work together to fight back. It tells me that we are all fellow humans."

He is ready to give a full sermon but then realizes that he'd better cut this short: "Of course, the guards would have succeeded to put the fire out by themselves sooner or later but with your help they did it faster. Now you can all go back to your cells, and in the morning, for breakfast we will distribute milk instead of tea. Good night to you all."

He is very proud; he just gave them the biggest reward.

Petros feels the intense urge to vomit, and cannot keep it down. He runs to the fountain and violently throws up. His stomach is empty now, but he still has the same urge. He washes his face and looks up. His glance rests on the window of the insane prisoner. Light smoke is still coming through the iron bars.

A guard approaches him.

"What is the matter with you?' he asks in a forceful manner.

"I felt nauseated, I don't know, but I feel better now."

"What upset you? Did you eat anything else besides the common meal?" He seems to think that nothing can happen to you if you eat the common meal.

Petros laughs at the idea.

"No, but it could be the smell of the burned body."

"Okay, if you are better now, go back to your position, or rather, to your cell. I see the others have already returned. Come, I'll get you there."

Petros walks back to his cell, and the guard follows behind him.

As they arrive at 322, the guard suddenly whispers to Petros: "Are you Professor Spathis?"

"Yes, and who are you?'

"Don't ask. I'm a guard. That's all you need to know. Do you need anything from outside? I go almost daily. Do you want me to bring you anything?"

His voice is clear, calm, low. Petros doesn't know what to tell him. Is this another little trap? Why does he all of a sudden want to help him?

Then he remembers his diary and decides to take the risk.

"I want some paper and two or three pens. Can you get them for me?"

"Sure, how much paper do you need?"

"Oh, get me a package, two hundred sheets."

"Alright, I will bring them to you the day after tomorrow with the evening meal, okay?"

"Thank you." Petros finds some money from his pocket and gives it to the guard.

The guard puts the money away and looks at Petros as though he was a fully bloomed rose, and the guard is ready to bend and smell it. But at once he comes back to his senses and motions Petros to go to his cell.

"Whatever we say must remain between us; otherwise, I will be in a lot of trouble. You must understand what my commander is like; he cannot even forgive his own mother."

"Don't worry."

"Okay then, good night."

"Good night to you too."

The guard locks Petros' cell door before he hurries away.

Again he is alone. The cellblock is deadly quiet. Then his ears slowly become aware of rhythmic knocks from the neighbor. He walks to his wall and tunes his ear to decipher the sequence. He grabs his paper and pen and quickly writes down the message: "Can you hear me 322? Can you hear me 322?"

Petros takes his dish and slowly puts together an answer, "I hear you, 321."

"Finally, I thought you have gone to sleep."

"What do you want?"
"Why are they holding you?"
"I don't know."
"Politics?" 321 insists.
"No."
"Not politics?"
"No."
"Murder?"
"No."
"Go to hell then. I thought that you were one of us."
"What you mean one of us?"
"Leftist, you fool."

Petros Spathis is stunned. He feels disgusted and doesn't want to say anything more. If Petros was a leftist and held for that reason, it would be a better person for 321. This is really the proof of how the great madness of the left and right still controls a man's behavior, even in the darkness of the prison cell. Left and right are the two opposing political views, yet they all want to achieve the same thing, Petros thinks; keep a man under the thumb of another man. The world works as a big chessboard and the big players move their armies against one another, and the majority of the people in the middle always pay the price with their lives.

It is very late, and he lies down on the bed. He is not aware of how long he spends thinking before sleep comes like a spider down the edge of night, and in a redeeming manner, takes him away.

13

The night is clear and bright. The stars in the sky manifest the depth of immensity and infinity, and the universe motions its greeting to the busy world of earth. The powers which hold the universe in its place are from the strong hand of the Creator. The people below have at their disposal other powers. They are busy exercising these powers against one another. For so many years, they have killed and been killed, they have cursed and been cursed instead of hugging one another and extending love to nature and its immense beauty. They destroy nature then hide when it revolts, spreading death in its passing. The bones of the dead sweat inside the graves, anxious to help maintain the peace which is carried away by a different kind of wind, high up in the air without ever stepping on this tortured earth.

Petros Spathis perches on the headboard of his bed to look through the iron-barred window. He stares at the sky. Since the evening meal, he has been here, maintaining the same position, with the same expressionless face. He looks at all this immensity and tries to pacify his mind by accepting solemnly whatever comes his way from the vastness of the universe and promises to see everything as a lesson and nothing more, a lesson from Him, the one full of kindness and forbearance.

He steps down from the bed, picks up his diary, and writes. The guard kept his promise and gave him the paper and pens. Petros forgets the date, but it doesn't matter; who cares what date it is? What does one more day mean? How can one measure the meaning of one more day in a prison cell? How may one day make any difference to the madness of infinity?

"All is created in wisdom and with concise precision: the earth with its snake-shaped rivers, its high mountains filled with snow, its valleys bathed in green, its lakes, trees, plants, animals, ravines in their immeasurable beauty, its seas with their crystal blue water, with their picturesque harbors and the immense oceans, with their richness and tranquility, with their storms and bitterness. All are showing His omnipotence. However, I don't see His omnipotence in man. People may say that his best creation is man who is His own image, yet I tell you: man is His worst deed. Perhaps He created man when He was asleep; He created man as a phantom to scare children and then allotted barbarous qualities to him as an excuse for all bloody murders committed over the eons by His best creation. People may say man carries the breath of God in him, yet I tell you, this breath stinks most of the times, just stinks. He sits on His red carpet, looking down and raising His eyebrows in horror, but He doesn't care enough to burn this creation of His and start from the very beginning. Centuries are gone by, day after day, passing like white or black clouds in the sky, yet his best creation still kills and maims in His name and in His whims. This is a sad state of affairs, I tell you."

He stops writing and looks at the text. His eyes hurt him his ears turn red along with his whole face. Sweat runs down his cheeks and forehead. He wipes it off, tensely, with the back of his hand.

He reads aloud what he wrote. The words seem unfamiliar. Who could have written them? Then a vague smile appears on his face. He has just written a letter to Him. He is angry with Him.

"Creation is a beautiful and rare jewel, and man is destroying it with his madness. Nature is pure and harmless, yet man kills all this with his insanity. All this freedom given to man is wasted in wars and killings; all this devastation in His name."

The pen in his hand gets stuck in the last word, and he cannot allow himself to carry on. He hides his head in his hands, and tears run down his cheeks; he cannot hold them back. Then he rips the paper into many pieces and throws it in the garbage. He wants to write something else. He picks up his pen and attempts to start again, but he cannot.

He gets up and starts pacing around his room, holding his hands behind his back and bowing his head down, watching every step of his feet. His shoes never leave the border of each stone as he walks.

He then gets bored. He sits on his bed, holds his hands up close to his chest and prays. After that, he lies down and tries to sleep. His thoughts don't let him, though, as they take him to his life before this dark cell, outside of these iron bars, outside his new enclave. Many a time he has judged himself, and many a time he has come to the same conclusion: there is nothing reprehensible in his behavior; he is not guilty of anything because he committed no wrong; just because his views are different from the governing clan, it doesn't mean that he committed a crime. Is he not a free man in a free society to express his views?

"Free man, free society?"

A funny voice laughs at him.

Sleep comes and takes him in its black arms, and his thoughts leave him alone to relax and dream of being free.

The next morning he wakes up as always from the noise of the military guard. He has no desire to get up, so he remains in bed and lights a cigarette. Then he changes his mind and jumps up. He wets his face. He steps onto the headboard of his bed and looks outside to see the weather. It is raining, drizzling calmly and lightly. Two drops fall on the hollow railing of the window and splash against the glass, making a soft sound. Hearing it, he shivers for a second, yet he begins to like the sound. There is a small aperture on the stone window ledge, and the water accumulates there. He promises himself to stay put until the thing is full of water. He keeps his eyes on it as the drops fall one by one and slowly create a small pool right in front of his eyes.

The guard's footsteps approach again as he goes around from cell to cell, giving out their morning beverage. Petros goes to his door and takes his share with a cold "thank you." The guard looks at him harshly and without any word walks away.

An hour later the same guard opens his door. He motions to Petros to follow him. Petros gets his jacket and steps out into the corridor.

"What is going on? Another questioning?" he wonders.

The guard pushes him lightly, pointing to him the same direction he had last time, the same route, the same quietness, the same water running in the same way underneath.

They stop outside the same small door after the underground journey. The guard knocks twice with his fist, and the door opens. The guard takes Petros in. It is the same room. The guard tells him to sit in the middle of the room, in the same chair underneath the same light, and then offers him a cigarette. They both light up, and after a couple of puffs, two officers enter. Petros recognizes the captain who interrogated him the first time. The other one must be his superior.

"Colonel, this is the prisoner 322, whose situation you are so familiar with," the captain says to the other officer.

"Thank you, Captain. Tell the prisoner to move his chair a bit forward."

The voice sounds so familiar; is it possible that Colonel Vikas is here?

Petros feels his heart beat faster and faster.

The captain's strict and commanding voice brings him back to reality.

"322, bring your seat forward."

He stands up and picks up his chair. Then he recognizes Colonel Vikas sitting at the desk, busy assessing a file, Petros' file. Petros freezes. Then he regains his composure and gets closer to his friend. Maybe it is better for Vikas if he shows that he doesn't know him.

The colonel lifts his eyes from the file and stares directly at Petros. His face tells Petros so much in a split second. None of the others present can imagine!

"Well, prisoner 322, how have you been keeping the past while?"

"I guess alright, Colonel," Petros utters.

"This prisoner is a very stubborn man, Colonel, if you know what I mean," says the captain.

"Yes, yes, I know very well, Captain. But do me a favor and leave me alone with him for a while."

"But, Colonel . . ." exclaims the captain.

"I think I have made myself clear, Captain. Leave me alone with the prisoner 322. I'll call you when I need you."

His voice has the weight of the order. The captain bends his head as he leaves the room with the guard.

Vikas and Petros are alone, just as other times, but this time in a different setting. Yet now, Vikas sits at the interrogator's chair, and Petros is his prisoner to be questioned.

"How are you? How are they treating you here?" the colonel asks Petros, and a tender concern is evident in his voice.

"Unfortunately, Colonel, things are not that great, and I'm afraid they are to get worse. But you, why are you here? Would it be dangerous for you if they know that we know each other?"

"Don't worry about me, Petros, I'll tell you all about it. Remember that pig, Alvarezos? He is the one behind all this. He managed to get transferred to the National Security Department and also to get me the commander's position here. He is trying to trap me into something. But don't worry; I'm so close to my retirement that he can't inflict any harm on me. On the other hand, he can do plenty of harm to you."

"You mean he is involved in what happened to me? I remember him when they arrested me at the school."

"The pig never liked you, especially after the night at the dean's house. They had your lectures bugged. They heard every word you ever said to your students. The man has the connections and the power to do these things; he used all these to get to us. He has you in a bad corner. They are actually accusing you of inciting rebellion and counterrevolutionary actions to undermine the security of the country. Do you know what that means? As long as they are in power, you may have to stay in prison. They don't follow any protocol or due process. He even had my son transferred here. He is a guard; you may have recognized him. He resembles me a lot."

Petros' memory goes back to the guard he thought he knew from someplace during the first interrogation session. Yes, it makes sense now. He must be Vikas' son. But why didn't he identify himself? Of course, Petros says to himself, he is a jail guard, and he has to follow his orders.

"Yes, that pig took care of everything; he even tries to corner me and my own son. You see, he will know at any time of anyone who helps you. But don't worry; old man Vikas knows his job well. Don't worry."

"I don't want get you into trouble, and even more, I don't want to get your son into trouble over my case," Petros tells his friend sincerely.

Vikas smiles lightly and continues, "Don't worry, Petros. There are still people who care. The first week of your arrest, I got a call from your TA, Amalia. I don't know how she found I know you, but these students of yours, they just find out everything they need to find out. They are the ones I'm worried about because they staged some demonstrations that publicized your case. You know, one day these kids will pay a price for it. They'll face files, records, and all that. This cruel dictatorship stops at nothing when it comes to their survival. And Amalia, what a girl! What a fire in her heart! I tell you these young people amaze me."

Petros feels a stabbing at his heart that is both painful and pleasing—oh, Amalia, Amalia.

"But I have done nothing wrong, Vikas."

"I know, Petros, I know, yet you remember I took your side in that evening gathering. Alvarezos didn't like that, same as he never liked you from the first day you got your job at the school. They have been following you step by step. I visited a couple of my old pals the other day, trying to plead your case, and one good ol' friend shut my mouth up by telling me that your ideas can cause riots, which in turn may become the ground for a civil war. Of course, I pay little attention to this idiotic thinking, but as I thought about it, I realized that it could be another reason why you are here. They can't do anything to me, but they can just take you out anytime."

Vikas sighs; then quickly changes his tone, "But Spathis, I'm sure, everything will go well. Don't worry. I'll take care of things. Now, how can I make your life a bit easier here?"

"You know, they don't even allow the guards to talk to me; it is amazing. They are really afraid of me. Thank you, though. I don't really need anything."

"Okay then. By the way, I'm here only two days a week; the rest of the time you are with them alone. This captain is a very stern man, and he only goes by the black book, nothing outside it. Now, when he comes in make sure your hands look like they're shaking when you light a cigarette. You know what I'm saying to you?"

Petros smiles at his suggestion.

"All right, Vikas, all right."

Vikas leaves, and in two minutes, he returns, escorted by the captain and the guard who remains at the door, looking at Petros closely.

"Can I smoke, Colonel?"

"Go ahead, prisoner."

The captain takes out his pack of cigarettes and offers one to Petros, and then, asking the colonel's pardon, turns and offers a cigarette to his superior who kindly refuses. Petros takes the cigarette. The captain offers him a light. Petros' hand starts to shake terribly. A satanic smile spreads over the captain's face. He doesn't return to his post behind the colonel but walks slowly around Petros, watching his every move and thinking, "how did this colonel make the prisoner shake like this? What did he say to him? He has been accused of being the prisoner's friend, yet what kind of a friend makes his friend frightened so much? "Vikas, you'd better be careful," the captain's mind goes, "this prisoner is already written off, and your turn is fast approaching. Everything is arranged to the smallest detail. They are only looking for the excuse to do away with you." The captain smiles sardonically. However, when his glance meets Vikas' intense stare, a shudder goes through his whole body.

Petros pretends he doesn't understand anything of this and keeps on smoking his cigarette. Two minutes of silence go by and the colonel turns to the guard.

"Take the prisoner to the next room. I need a few moments with the captain."

"Yes, Sir," the guard salutes, and Petros gets up and follows him to the next room. About half an hour later, he hears footsteps in the hall, and then the captain appears at the door.

"Guard, bring the prisoner back."

Without a word, the guard escorts Petros to the interrogation room. Vikas is gone. The prisoner's chair is moved in the middle of the room, underneath the light. The captain motions him to sit there and orders the guard to leave.

When they are alone, the captain walks around Petros' chair, keeping a distance from him so that he can see the prisoner clearly. Then, suddenly, he takes a big step closer to Petros and hisses.

"Listen, prisoner, listen, 322, or Professor Spathis, I'm not impressed with your friendship with Colonel Vikas. Don't deny the fact that you are good friends. However, no matter how many colonels may help you, you are not getting out of here unless you tell me all I want to hear."

He is sharp and sadistic. For the first time, he called Petros by name. Petros feels nauseated.

"I'm listening, prisoner. What was all this about a united Europe that you promoted to your students during your lecture the second of October?"

"I said nothing wrong. This has nothing to do with what you have me here for and you know it. I'm innocent. Put me to trial and you'll see that my innocence will be proven."

"I see that you believe in justice a lot, 322, but understand this: there may be no trial."

Petros shivers at these words. "The only thing I can tell you is that I am innocent. I have nothing more to say."

"It seems you haven't wised up yet. Let me show you something that will convince you that we know every single move you have made."

The captain walks over to the guard and whispers in his ear.

The guard leaves the room, and two minutes later, he returns, holding a box. The captain lights a cigarette.

"Do you know what's in this box?"

Petros shakes his head. The captain opens the box and takes out a tape recorder. He plugs it in and pushes the on button.

"Well, listen carefully, prisoner 322."

The tape winds slowly, and Petros' curiosity arises.

"Since the end of the Second World War, our country, along with a few others in this area called the Balkans, is struggling under the manipulation of foreign interests. We are seemingly free to direct the destiny of our people, but if we want to be honest with ourselves, we must admit that we do absolutely nothing without the approval of these foreign interests. We are free slaves, literary speaking. We belong to the Atlantic Alliance, but that does not give us the right to demand things or to make a move without first asking for approval of another country, in this case, the United States of America."

Petros now remembers this discussion in his class, yes, October the second. But why is this reason for his arrest?

"We live under an oppressed system," the voice carries on before the captain angrily shuts the tape recorder off.

"Which 'oppression' do you mean 322? That of the Americans or the military rule? What do you suggest by that to your students? To go out and demonstrate, is this your solution?"

Petros' face reddens, but manages to say calmly, "I don't suggest anything to them. I just state the facts based on my personal observations of our history after the second War."

"Well, listen to what comes after, 322. Let me see what you mean further on," the captain shouts and turns the recorder on again.

"We can change this situation by extending the effect of the United Europe concept. We are already part of the European Union; if this Union also becomes a military power, we may be able to stand up to the influence of the Americans, and we can master our affairs in a better way. After all, we are Europeans and belong to Europe, not the United States."

The captain again shuts the recorder and retorts, "A United Europe, 322? Would you like it to be in the format of the USSR? Why not turn to communism while we are at it?" he stops to breathe, then continues, "Is that what you like us to become? A satellite of the Soviets? Like the Bulgarians and the Serbs?"

"I never suggested that, Captain. My discussion is simply a theoretical one and points to the perils of us following international political situations which are detrimental most of the time. My views are simply nationalistic, and I care for the well being of all Hellenes."

The captain looks at him with a forced smile.

"A United Europe, eh?"

"I see nothing wrong with it. I am not opposing my own views."

"You are not in any position to judge, prisoner, whether your suggestion is good or bad or whether it opposes our views. We judge, you do not."

"Don't I even have the right to judge my own actions or ideas?"

"You don't even have the right to ask any questions, 322. I have made this quite clear to you already. But let us leave this aside for a while. Let me ask you: why didn't you ever consult the government trustee at the school to ask what is proper material to discuss in class before you went out there and threw it to the students?"

Petros looks at him and realizes it is about who calls the shots and nothing more; they may let him go if he agrees to sign their beloved document of sell out.

"I never asked for approval from the trustee because I didn't see it as necessary. I was supposed to have complete freedom in what I teach. That was my understanding with the dean."

"Without any exception, you behaved like a revolutionary."

"I hope you don't mean it when you call me a revolutionary, Captain. After all, you consider your own government revolutionary. Or have you already forgotten the way by which you acquired power?"

"This is none of your business, prisoner."

Petros feels the need to laugh every time he hears these evasive replies.

The captain gets up and starts his pacing again around Petros' seat.

"Anything else you need to tell me, 322? Before you rush to an answer, remember there are a few tapes of this kind, and nothing is hidden from us. So, is there anything else you have to say?" he repeats.

"No, I have nothing to tell you. It seems you already know it all and you have also established your idea of what is there for me to say," Petros shoots, and that shuts the captain off.

They remain silent for a while, and then the captain orders the guard to take him back to his cell.

Petros gets up. He looks at the captain once more as the man gathers his papers from the desk and puts them away in his briefcase. They say nothing else. He is escorted back to his cell. His door closes. The guard locks Petros' door and the sound of his footsteps slowly fade away.

Petros sits on his bed, lights a cigarette. His mind goes to Vikas. He also tries to straighten things up in his mind. He remembers all his lectures and knows there is nothing indicating that he is guilty of anything. Yet they have marked him out.

He pushes his bed under the window and climbs onto the headboard. The sky is cloudy and dark. He feels the need to have a conversation, to say something, to let everything out, to release himself of his thoughts. His mind goes to his neighbor. He moves to the wall, but then changes his mind: better leave this man alone. Yet he feels choking, his breath becomes heavy, his throat closes, and his mind turns dim. He wants to talk to someone, to say something, to live. Yet he is alone in the loneliness of a cell with the number 322 on its door. He paces up and down faster and faster as if he wanted to run away from the four walls and his mind kills his peace as the frustration builds up. He simply becomes as numb as the rusted nails which barely hold things together. A rusted nail, a rusted man, and a rusted dream, all rusted.

He looks outside again: a whole world is out there, yet his world is just inside this cell, 322, a number he didn't choose. Who chose this number for the young professor Petros Spathis? Was it fate or a well-schemed plan by a bunch of executioners who only care for the suppression of people's freedom in order to stay in power for the longest time?

He is not aware of how long he has been standing there, and his feet start hurting him. He gets down and finds his diary to write a few words.

Perhaps he needs to write everything down, so if something happens to him, his students will someday find it and understand where his views have taken him. He tries to start but can't get going. He looks at the paper and pushes his pen against it as if the pen were to do the writing on its own. He pushes the pen so hard that the paper rips. He throws the pen and the paper across the cell, then lies down in bed and remains still for a long while until the tension slowly goes away.

14

He used to etch one mark on the wall for each day. Now, his days go by without him remembering to count them anymore. Light comes every morning and goes away every night, and Petros Spathis, prisoner 322, realizes that life behind the walls is a different kind of a fruit, one which cannot be eaten no matter how much the person intends to try. Sometimes he wonders whether it has been a month, a year, or a century since he was jailed. He can't help asking, "Are they going to do the inevitable one day?" "Will it be in daylight or the darkness of the night? Or will it be under a full moon?" He feels like an injured animal attracting the predators—the hyenas are closing in, smelling the blood. The condors fly gracefully on top of the clouds, and Petros Spathis is nothing else but the quarry.

He talks to nobody other than the prisoner in the next cell, who at times gives him a break from the monotonous rhythm of his dish hitting the wall.

Today he wakes up a bit more cheerfully, having a presentiment that everything is going to be just fine. This pleasant feeling just appeared this morning, and it is the reason why he is up so early from his bed, even before the guards make their morning rounds. Sitting on the bed, he allows himself to sink into his thoughts, and then a voice from the corridor comes and shocks him: "Spathis, reveille."

He jumps from his bed and runs to the door.

He doesn't know how long he has been standing there but his bare feet are freezing. He returns to his bed and tries to lie down and then changes his mind. Yes, of course, he heard it right: "Spathis, reveille." He gets dressed in a hurry, washes his face, and shaves. He even cleans his dish. Is the voice going to talk to him again? His heart twinges pleasantly at the thought, yet he doesn't like to feed himself false hopes. His temples pound loudly. A little longer in this place and insanity will get hold of him for sure. One thousand questions go through his mind to which he finds one thousand and more uncertain answers.

He sits on the bed and keeps his eyes on his door. Any second now it will open so the guard can pass him his tea. He feels he must do something. He raises his hand and with his finger pointing at the door he claims: "I am Professor Petros Spathis."

The words painfully ring in his ears. He gets up and touches the small window on the door. He pushes it with his thumb, hard, with all his strength as if to make a hole: he is going to get out, to be free. "Spathis, your tea," says a voice. Sharp. Clipped. But even so he feels in it something so warm, so humane so alive. He stands still, staring at the now half-opened door. A guard dips a ladle into the cauldron of tea, and holds it out for Petros' cup, dripping some tea on the floor. The guard is puzzled; he puts the ladle back in the caldron, opens the door wider, and looks inside.

"Spathis, your tea."

The prisoner jumps, wakes up, comes back to life and smiles at the young man by the door.

"Did you just talk to me?"

"Yes, come and get your tea."

The eyes of the guard are black, his hair the same, his forehead wide, his nose and mouth big. He is very tall and well built. Petros takes his ladleful of tea in his cup, and the bread and eight olives on his plate. The door closes again.

Petros Spathis walks to his bed. He sits and carefully places his plate and tea on the bed as though they were holy. He tears a chunk from his bread with his hand and dips it in the tea. The tea tastes better today, and the olives appear to be a lot bigger than before. He then sits for a long time, contemplating the olives; eight of them, sixteen bites. Finally, he grabs them in one handful and eats them with great appetite. He finishes eating and lights his sacred cigarette. He smokes it down to the butt in between his two fingers squeezing the end of it. After the last puff, he throws it to the other side of the cell; it hits the wall and falls on the floor. He gets up and steps on it, then bends down to blow the ashes away and throws the end of the cigarette in the waste basket. He goes back to his bed with nothing more to do. How is it that he has nothing to do? He pulls his bed under the window again, gets on top of the headboard and looks outside in the courtyard: the same guard, the same pavement, the same fountain in the middle, and the window of the mad man still there, black from the fire. He gets down and pulls the bed back to its place. Maybe it is time to write his diary again.

He turns the paper to a new page, although he finished the last entry in the middle of the previous page. He wants to enter the date on top, but what is the date today?

"Today something unexpected occurred. The guard called me by my name. I cannot remember exactly how long it's been since they arrested me, but today for the first time I noticed a different behavior from the guard. I suspect that Vikas is the reason for this. Perhaps the justice I have been waiting for may eventually come."

He stops writing, his mind weakening, offering him nothing more. He reads what he just wrote, then again, and again. He closes his diary and puts it away.

An hour goes by slowly and softly as Petros sits in the same position on his bed; his heartbeat keeps him company, as well as his thoughts, which always haunt him.

His ears hear voices. He gets up on the headboard and looks outside. The prisoners are on their usual morning walk. About twenty of them walk up and down the yard in small groups, talking and sometimes yelling. There are two guards on each side of the courtyard, and perhaps another two on the other two sides of the courtyard whom Petros can't see from where he is. He wonders whether the prisoners are in prison for political reasons, like him, or they are criminals. But if they are criminals, why are they in the same prison as he?

His eyes catch three tall men and a short one talking. The short guy talks with his hands going a mile a minute; his mannerisms show that he is angry about something. If Petros pays more attention, he will probably understand what the short man is yelling about. They are all white on their faces, and their hands pale. He imagines that he is probably as pale as they. How long has it been since last he saw the sun outside? How long has it been since he saw the brightness of the sky outside of this cursed cell?

Well, he got arrested on October 13th, but what is the date today? He cannot remember. He hears the bell ring from the courtyard in a sad tone, and he sees the guards leading the prisoners toward the big door. It seems that the daily walk is over. A minute later the courtyard will be deserted, empty as before, with only the fountain in the middle and the black colored window of the mad man on the other side.

The sound of boots is down the corridor. The familiar jingle of keys, one of them turns the lock of his door, and the guard, the same one who talked to him this morning, appears in the frame of the door.

"Spathis, come, it is time for your walk."

Petros Spathis cannot believe what he hears.

"You mean that I can go for a walk in the yard?"

"Yes, Spathis, the order is clear, half an hour of a daily walk for you."

The professor is convinced that this is a new thing, and he doesn't want to waste any time with silly questions. He puts on a light coat and follows the guard into the courtyard. Then the guard stands aside, and Petros is alone, walking around and around to enjoy the wind and the sky.

There are two exits to the yard from inside the prison. One is the double door they came through, and the other one, smaller, on the opposite side. There are two levels of cells above ground. One section on the first floor has bigger windows. He assumes those are the warden's offices. Watch-posts are at the four corners of the yard, and barbed wire fences stretch out along the top of the walls. He examines all these as he walks. Then he looks at the sky, the lonely sky. The day is dark; clouds cover the sun, casting gloom over the earth.

The guard in the opposite corner sneezes and takes out a handkerchief to blow his nose. Petros walks toward the guard, and then changes his mind and walks toward the fountain. He turns on the tap and bends to drink some water. As he stands up, his glance instinctively falls on the charred window of the mad man. He turns away and takes a cigarette out from his pack and lights it. He takes a deep puff and blows the smoke high. He doesn't know what else he wants to do.

At last the guard motions to him to get inside. They enter through the wider door to the narrow corridors with weak light and complete silence. He wants to ask something although he knows he shouldn't.

"Can I ask you what the date is today?"

The guard is surprised but replies politely.

"The second of November."

No other word is spoken. When they reach 322 the guard opens the door, Petros goes inside to his cosmos. He grabs the diary and writes: "2nd of November."

He has been imprisoned for less than a month. What is happening to the people outside, and how do they cope with all this? Samantha, what happened to her? Amalia and his students, what happened to them? Magda, how is her life these days?

Life moves on with the new rhythm. Every morning at twelve, after all the other prisoners return to their cells, he gets to walk for half an hour in the courtyard. At least now he can admire the blue sky whenever possible. He also notices the light moss growing in the cracks of the wall. Nature always finds a way to create life, no matter where it is.

He sits on his bed with his legs crossed in a yoga position and writes his diary. The pen travels over the white paper, making shapes of letters, words, phrases, and an immense eagle flying in the sky.

Petros Spathis is following his deeper self to a mysterious world where he sees only beauty and joy. In such moments his soul soars in the vastness of his blue sky like a phantasmal eagle which outlines the path of purity in a simple and redeemed fashion.

But then his pen stops. His creative images freeze like marionettes in the hands of a master who abruptly stops; a plethora of sharp knives aim at his heart. His eyes turn toward the window. Two horizontal iron bars and three vertical ones cut the blue sky into twelve small pieces.

"Deliverance! What form will it take? What time will it show up? Is it possible that I have just missed it?"

His ears catch some conversation coming from the courtyard. He pulls his bed under the window and climbs on the headboard. Yes, many people, men and women, are in the courtyard. It must be Sunday. The prisoners get to embrace their wives, their children, their friends, with tears in the eyes. They get to laugh and talk. Time goes by faster now. Soon one of the guards walks into the middle of the yard, a sign that the visiting time is over. He blows his whistle, and the visitors give their loved ones one last hug and last kiss before they make their way toward the exit. The whistle goes one more time, and the visitors leave. All is quiet again.

Petros comes down from the headboard and lights a cigarette. He isn't yet halfway through it when footsteps start in the corridor. Then his door opens, and the guard appears with a warm smile.

"Spathis, follow me."

Petros Spathis gets his thin jacket, and before they go, he can't hold himself back anymore: "Do I know you? You look so familiar."

"It is I who should apologize, Professor. I'm Demetre Vikas; you know my father."

"Yes, this is how I thought I knew you. You look like your father. Thank you. But what is going on today? Where am I going?"

"You have a visitor, Professor."

The young man motions for Petros to go. Petros quickly starts to walk, and Demetre follows behind him according to the protocol.

When they reach the courtyard, Petros opens his eyes wide to look for his visitor, his heart beating faster and faster.

"Petros, Petros," he hears his name called and immediately recognizes the Canadian accent.

There, Samantha is in the courtyard a few meters away from him. Not believing his eyes, he turns to her and she falls in his arms. He finds her lips and glues his to them, so warm and so soft. This is what he had missed most.

Is he dreaming? Could this be real? How could they allow her in here?

Samantha is crying, and he kisses her eyes. He holds her tight, very tight, fearing that time will go by so quickly that soon she is going to go away. How he wishes time will freeze! This moment should be made an eternity.

"It is really you, Samantha?" he still can't trust his own eyes, but she nods her head and looks deep into his eyes with unlimited happiness: she has so many things to tell him.

"Yes, I managed. I am so happy to see you!"

She tells him all: her dealings with the Canadian embassy, her father's crucial effort of getting the marriage certificate, her hope that as a husband and wife they'll go back to Vancouver as soon as he is free.

Petros Spathis is stunned with all this unexpected news, good news, and strange news, especially the part about how she managed to convince the Canadian embassy that they are married. Samantha tells him that even Magda agreed to help by signing herself as a witness of their marriage.

"My dad knows a lot of people, Petros. You know that. He can do things when he needs to. The Canadian embassy people say they may be able to help us. Now tell me how you are. Have they tortured you?"

"No, they have not. Let's find a more private place." He takes her hand in his and they make their way around the yard. They find the corner where the smaller door is, leading them inside. Petros stops there and hugs Samantha again. They kiss and his blood wants to burst out. He lets his hands go inside her dress and feel the smoothness of her skin.

"Oh, Sam, oh, how I missed you!"

Samantha lets his hands find every spot of her body he wants to touch and knows he wants to just touch her everywhere. Petros leans against the frame of the door and turns his back to the direction of Demetre, who sees them and knows what is about to happen. He turns to face the other side of the courtyard and lights a cigarette.

Samantha gets closer to him and kisses him with passion. She is so excited about having him right here in this prison courtyard. She leans against the frame of the door and takes his hand and puts it between her legs while sliding his zipper down. She takes his firmness in her hand and lifts her left leg high, opening the way for him. She then pulls her panties on the side, and he is finally inside her. In two or three strokes he releases all his sexual hunger. For a moment he feels like he is in heaven.

"Oh, Sam, oh, God, oh, Sam," he cries and holds her tighter.

They soon realize where they are, and Samantha quickly fixes herself while he zips himself up. They start walking again around the yard. He tells her how his time is spent in jail, mostly of his diary writing, his good news about getting a walk everyday after all the other prisoners are gone...

He notices this deep sadness in her eyes. His heart tightens, "My love, you should go back to Canada. I can't keep you here for me."

"I love the idea of going back home, but I won't leave without you. Petros, I love you so much." She hugs him again.

"Don't say anything, Samantha. The fact that you are here tells me everything. I love you more than you can imagine. My life is yours."

This is the first time she hears him saying these words.

They both feel their hearts are closer than ever. They say nothing more, only to enjoy those moments together. Then, a concern for her safety comes to his mind, and all calmness disappears.

"I'm worried about you, Samantha. Coming here makes you a target for the people who do not like me, you know."

"Oh, don't worry, honey. I'm a Canadian citizen, nobody can touch me. Believe me."

Her eyes glitter with happiness and joy as she relates to him in more detail what happened at the embassy and how the clerk helped her. He is really pleased with how she managed to get their marriage certificate.

"I'll come and visit you next Sunday."

At that time, Demetre Vikas signals for them to come over. "The visiting hour is over, prisoner," the guard says in a loud and sharp voice. Then he leans closer and whispers, "The girl has to go, sir."

"Alright, my boy," Petros nods to Demetre and turns to Samantha. "I love you, Sam. Don't worry about me too much. Everything will be okay. You'll see."

He says these words with an effort to convince himself as well as Samantha. She smiles at him and kisses him once more.

"I'll see you again next week."

She goes, and he stays there looking at her as she disappears behind the double door. He is alone in the courtyard again. He walks to the fountain and bends to splash some water over his face and drinks some as well.

"Time to go inside, 322," Demetre Vikas says loudly.

Petros notices that the warden's window is open; perhaps an official heard them, perhaps even saw them. He walks ahead, and the guard follows close behind through the corridors. They get to 322. Vikas unlocks the door and says to Petros, "I'm sorry I had to talk to you aloud outside. You know the rules."

"I know, don't be bothered, I know. How is your father doing?"

"He is fine, and he sends his regards to you. Are they treating you okay?"

"Good enough, I suppose. What is your father worrying about?"

"I don't know, but he is planning to come and see you soon, he says."

"Okay, Demetre, you probably have to go now. Thank you for your help."

"I'm on duty twice a week. If you need anything from outside, do not hesitate to tell me."

"Thank you, thank you. But I'm good. Go now before you get into trouble over my affairs."

The guard locks the prisoner inside his cell and leaves.

An intense sadness overcomes Petros when he thinks of Samantha and the news from Demetre Vikas. He lights a cigarette and starts pacing with his head down and his thoughts pounding his temples.

"One more day in this cursed cell for no reason at all," he writes. "Who knows how many more days I will have to spend here? No one knows; no one tells me. I hear nothing about an upcoming trial. Are they going to try me or keep me here for as long as they want? Are they ever going to let me go?"

He shivers at the thought and stops writing for a while. Then he takes the pen again.

"Vikas, I see now that you care for my safety so much. But for how long will you be able to help me and protect me? But, no matter what happens, remember that Petros Spathis never bends. I know it is the same with you."

He turns the page and carries on . . .

"Today is my most pleasant day here. Samantha came to visit me. A great effort on her part, a great proof of her love; yet I fear for her safety. I'm afraid I'll never be able to give her the happiness she deserves."

He closes the diary and starts pacing around the cell again.

The sound of footsteps arises from the corridor. It must be time for the noon meal. He grabs his dish and waits for the door to open. Today's lunch includes potatoes with pork, an apple, a boiled egg, and some bread. He takes one bite of the potato; it is actually appetizing. He eats heartily and goes to lie down. His thoughts return to keep him company, but sleep finds him and he is gone.

15

Far off in the distance, he can hear the sound of church bells so clearly that it reaches his ears like a song of new hope. It must be Sunday today. Samantha is coming today. This thought gets him up from his bed in a flash, and he goes to his sink where he cleans, shaves, and brushes his teeth.

Vikas' son is on duty today. While giving Petros his morning tea, Demetre confirms that it is indeed Sunday. He enjoys his breakfast better than any other day he can remember. After cleaning his dish, he becomes restless. He has to find something to do until she comes to visit. Oh God, what an experience he had with her last Sunday! How about those students of his? How are they coping with all the things which happened lately? Did they get into trouble? Samantha came to visit, why not his parents, or his uncle and auntie, or Magda? Perhaps the warden doesn't allow them, or perhaps they are too afraid to try.

His neighbor from 321 starts a new conversation with Petros; he taps on the wall try to convince Petros that if he turns to their political side of the left, he is going to have plenty to gain. Petros pities this stubborn man. But isn't Petros Spathis the same? After all, he is in a cell for his views and beliefs too. So Petros finds himself more and more like the man tapping the dish against the wall.

Often Petros exchanges a few words with Demetre Vikas when he is on duty. This allows Petros to know what is happening outside, and be informed on how the colonel is doing. This morning, Demetre tells Petros that the colonel is coming to visit him soon and may bring some good news. Optimism and enthusiasm sweep through Petros. He sits and writes his daily entry, knowing that this detail of what goes through his mind everyday may be very useful to him at some time in the future. He then sits on his bed and counts the stones which make up the wall across from him. There are 216 stones on one wall and 864 stones therefore on all four walls. Subtracting the opening space of the door, which amounts to 36 stones, he then gets a total of 828 stones. He can write a short story about this and title it "UNDER THE CARE OF 828 STONES." He laughs a loud laugh.

The church bells invite the faithful to the sermon, and his love to his cell. He gets up and pulls his bed under the window to look at the courtyard. His eyes try to see beyond the walls and find the church, but without success. Yet the sound of the bells still echoes and gives him hope.

It is a bright sunny day. A couple of sparrows are playing around the fountain. Petros' eyes eagerly follow their flutters. *Today she is coming to visit me again.* This thought jumps out, and right away he starts his morning exercise. He likes to keep himself in good shape. His day of release is coming: he can feel it. He starts with his regular jumping rhythmically: he inhales deeply and exhales slowly. 828 stones against a man and the fight is unfair; yet he is going to win, and 828 stones will be defeated.

"Ha, ha, ha . . ." he laughs again.

He sits on his bed and grabs his diary again to write, "She begs to get her permit to come and visit me. How can I make this woman happy when I'm out of these walls? Best for me to go back to Vancouver until the situation here changes. Vancouver, what a nice city with all its clean air and all its greens! Yes, I like the idea; I'll go back with Samantha and live in Vancouver, at least for a while."

The hours of his morning go by smoothly. He is pacing in his cell when voices, laughter, and greetings come to his ears. He pulls his bed under the window and looks at the courtyard. Visitors are in the yard with the prisoners, same ones as last week. All of them seem to be having fun with their relatives and friends.

Suddenly, a hysterical laugh flares up from his guts, and he can't stop laughing. It is so loud that a couple of visiting women turn and stare at him, whose face is clearly visible from his window. One of the prisoners shakes his head as if to say to his visitors, "Don't worry. He is just one more who cracked up. Just another sane man turned insane."

One of the women points at him, and Petros extends his hand behind the iron bars of the window and points back at her. She then puts her hand down and bites her lip.

He stays up there for a while until his feet become tired. Nothing more to do. The beats of his heart keep him company as he walks around the cell with his feet never going over the edges of the stones on the floor.

A whistle blows, and he goes to the window. The visitors are leaving and now it is his turn. Is Samantha here already?

He grabs his diary and writes quickly the incident of the woman pointing at him and him pointing at the woman. He adds: "I laughed so much today. What a strange behavior. Am I going crazy?"

The visiting hour is over, and the prisoners are back in their cells. He hears the sound of boots in the corridor. Yes, it is his turn now. The sound gets closer, and then the lock of his door turns. The face of young Vikas appears.

"322, you have visitors."

"Visitors?" Petros is surprised by the plural form.

"Yes, Sir," the young man whispers, "lots of them."

He jumps up as if he were electrocuted. Samantha must be here, but who else? He is almost runs to the yard. Demetre follows his fast steps and watches Petros as he is stunned by the crowd: Amalia and many of his students. Petros' legs weaken with emotion. He runs to them, hugs Amalia first, then all the others, Antoniou being the last on the line.

They are all smiling.

"I'm speechless. Thank you all for coming. How are your studies? How is life at school?"

Antoniou takes the lead and briefs the professor about what happened after they arrested him. Their lives are a bit different in the class without Petros. The trustee and a couple of plainclothes ask various questions. Other than that, everything is more or less okay. They have a few things they are pursuing, and around the middle of November something big is going to happen and affect their affairs in a big way.

"What is to happen?"

The young man whispers to him.

"A major undertaking is in the works, and it involves the polytechnic school student union along with us and a few others. This is going to shake the government's foundation, and nothing is going to save them. You'll see. This is the beginning of their end."

Petros is skeptical: "You have to be very careful. You see what happens to the ones they don't like? I don't want you to end up in a place like this one. Even your presence here could put you in a bad position."

"We understand, Professor," Antoniou says, "but do not worry about us. We know what we are doing."

They chat about various things for a while, and the time flies by. He finds out that the dean has been replaced, but the trustee is still there.

Demetre Vikas comes closer to give Petros the signal that it is time for them to go.

They promise to visit again, and he is really happy. They say goodbye one by one and walk toward the exit. Amalia hugs him and kisses him on his lips.

"I love you. Be patient. Things are going to change. Soon you'll be free and with us again."

He smiles at her, and her face lightens up as if a strong sun hit it for the first time. She goes, too, and he stands there watching her until she disappears behind the double doors. He goes back to his cell with young Vikas behind him.

He is alone and lonely again; he has nothing but the pain of being behind these walls, without the people he cares so much for.

Two days later, when distributing the evening meal, young Vikas comes to tell Petros that the colonel is coming to visit him this week.

After Petros finishes his meal, he sits on his bed and writes his diary.

The familiar knocking of a dish on the wall arrives right after he finishes his writing. Petros takes his own dish and codes an answer, "I hear you, 321."

"Out. Tomorrow."

"Who? How?"

"Two others. And I. Arranged."

"Explicit."

"No details now. Come or not."

"When? When?"

"Night."

Petros spins the roulette wheel of options, then answers, "Need space for thought. Definite reply tomorrow morning."

"Agreed. Watch your ass. I know the other two. If plans blow, we will know you are responsible."

"I have no taste for trouble, from any quarter."

"Have no taste for your sort. You intellectuals hide in ivory towers and have never even experienced life but you pretend to teach everyone about it. Wouldn't trust you to carry my garbage. Only because I know you were set up, like so many others, is why we invite you come."

"Your prejudice is admirably honest. Why are you here?"

"Because am not somewhere else."

"Very well. Thank you for the thoughtful invitation."

The signals cease, and Petros Spathis sits still as a duck hiding her nest among the reeds. He is attempting to unbraid the whorls and snarls of responsibility.

Two doors of action open for him: leave with the three prisoners and be outlawed with them, or stay? If the other two are friends of 321, it's certain all three are of the same political persuasion.

He has considered consummation of just such a political form, and now, here it is before him. He has but to declare his allegiance and begin translation of his abstruse learning into practical civil action. But the machine of fantasy falters as he remembers he has virtually no knowledge of 321, and none whatsoever of the other two. They can be authentic criminals or military spies sent to draw him out only to kill him for attempted escape. On the other hand, it might be his only chance. He could dissemble joining them and then escape, and find Samantha and fly to Vancouver before they even sniff of his going.

But, what about his followers? What about Samantha, who even lied about their marriage to the Canadian embassy? What about his students who are tireless in their efforts and Amalia with all her love for him? His credibility would be shattered. Vikas is calling upon all his resources to extricate him, too.

But if he does not leave, if the efforts of all his friends come to nothing, if Vikas' influence proves ineffectual, if this room becomes the only world in which he is fated to participate from here on; possibly his guilt has been decided long before his incarceration, as there is no forthcoming trial in the docket.

All these thoughts swirl between his temples and torture his sanity. He decides to leave things for tomorrow. In the morning his thoughts will be clear. He lights a cigarette. Soon wrapped in aromatic smoke, his bedeviled thought, and a blanket, he sinks to sleep, half-dreaming of better things to come.

The following morning the guard doesn't need to knock on his door to wake him up; he has already been up for a while. He sits in his usual manner on the bed with his diary.

Date ... November 18th ... Time ... He doesn't need to look at his watch—the guards are doing their rounds. His days are measured according to the footsteps of the guards: the distribution of the breakfast, the noon meal, the evening meal, and the walk in the courtyard. There is an order in this cursed place. "Today asks of me a significant decision. I haven't had the opportunity to employ my mental machinery for so long. Perhaps it has fallen into ill repair or atrophied since this room first cleft me from freedom. I have grown unaccustomed to decision-making. This imprisonment has, until today, provided not only all the answers, but all the questions as well. At this degree of predestined uncertainty, thought is at best an empty exercise ... Acknowledge your agonist Kyrie ... I ask only the strength to decide. A decisive act, a refusal perhaps . . . To escape is to opt for the fugitive . . . Always I would be looking over my shoulder. Is it I who is to remain and become the exemplary victim?"

Petros feels the terror of a cornered animal. He can almost smell the reek of fear exuding from his pores, the unmistakable stench given off by a beast profound in fright. The blunt voice from the dark current of brute survival commands him: "You cannot afford the risk of remaining with only a sliver of hope for company. Go with them, because so many draw strength from you. You must deny yourself the luxury of death. Go with them."

He springs up like as gazelle ready to run across the open field. His mind is made up. He grabs his plate.

"321, do you hear me?"

"Yes. Decision."

"Coming with you."

"Excellent."

"Plan."

"Tonight someone will open your door. Follow. He will bring you to us."

"And then."

"Never mind."

"Go where?"

"Patience. You will soon find out all you need to know."

The conversation is cut short by the sound of the guard approaching with breakfast. Petros receives his and eats merrily. Today, he has a genuine appetite.

He sits silently through the transit of the next hours. They curve and flow around him like a slow sea wind around the bole of an olive tree.

"Done. It is done. I'm committed now. Consummation of valence . . . Totally irrational, totally absolute, Kyrie Kierkegaard, I have made your leap. It is a difficult matter for a scholar to learn that in an irrational time the reason is ornamental rather than functional. Storms of unreason can only be met on their own terms. Tonight is night of the opening door, tonight of the liberation. As this room dictates all questions and all answers now, flight as an outlaw will provide exactly the same service. Follow? Whom? They must have purchased a guard. The only plausible explanation . . ."

Brisk officious footsteps sound outside Petros' door, which opens to reveal a guard who radiates self-importance and military authority.

"Spathis, get ready. You have visitors."

The prisoner snatches up his jacket and goes through the door. The guard escorts him to the courtyard. The enclosure is empty. Petros looks toward the guard in bewilderment. The guard shrugs then takes up sentry on the courtyard side of the door. Petros is left to walk laps around the courtyard, observing the ground beneath his pass with each step. When he looks up, Colonel Vikas materializes from the smaller door. He is dressed in civilian garb, smiling.

"Good morning, Professor 322."

"Good morning, Colonel," he says as he shakes Vikas' hand, then whispers to him, "Have you lost your mind? By associating with me in the open, you could lose your life. Your career is at stake, your freedom. If anything happens to you, it will be my fault."

"Shhh, Spathis, don't ask me any questions, and don't say anything, just listen. We have half an hour for me to brief you. You are going to be freed. Your troubles will soon end. Arrangements are not completely concluded, however. I have a few contacts among the ministers. I have convinced them of your case. The only official remaining is the Prime Minister who I have an appointment with the day after tomorrow. I feel certain he won't dare to oppose the consensus of his ministers."

Petros is euphoric.

"The news is just too unexpected for me to contain myself!"

"How are they treating you?"

"Well enough, I suppose. It was unpleasant before the second interrogation, but thereafter everything changed. The guards exchange a few words with me now. I also have a half-an-hour walk in this courtyard alone each day. I've had visitors a couple of times, but I'm afraid they place themselves in jeopardy when they associate with me. For these few privileges I know you are responsible. I feel deeply grateful."

"All that is beside the way; the objective now is your release from this cage and complete reinstatement of your rights, insofar as rights are possible at all under this barbaric regime. Be patient in the knowledge that your day of freedom is near. Your students are nothing short of astonishing. They are tireless in their efforts to campaign for your freedom. Yesterday, the students of the polytechnic school took a major action. Unfortunately yesterday became a dark day in the history of our country."

"What happened?"

"There had been an uprising in the polytechnic school grounds for the last few days. Yesterday, the government ordered the army tanks onto the school grounds. The gates were crashed and the students arrested. A great number of them are jailed, and the political situation changed for the worse. The few civil liberties given back to the people the last few months are now taken away. The government has changed to a more forceful dictatorship, just like the early days, back in 1967. A new prime minister has appointed himself to power."

Petros Spathis is speechless.

"What about my students? Are they arrested?"

"I don't know yet. I'm looking into it, but the situation is just so grim. However, I do salute their courage and dedication. Now, I'm going to answer some of the questions you have probably asked yourself over and over all this time. Someday that beast, Alvarezos, will pay for all this. However there has been a file on you since the time you visited your parents on the island before leaving to do your graduate work abroad. Without a doubt, you had said something in a conversation that an official overheard and disagreed with. The government does not usually investigate such incidents so closely. Think back now: who might have reported you?"

Petros sends the bucket down deep into the well-filled cistern of the past and draws it up: "My own village? The mayor of my village?

Who else has the energy to start such a thing? Have the reserves of trust in the world been depleted already? Can any man not be purchased?"

"No, and all who are working to extricate you are proof enough."

"Of course, forgive me."

"In any case, the story begins on the island and leads to the trap they set for you in which you eventually fell. The dean's home provided the scenario for episode number two. Another black mark."

"But I said nothing seditious."

"That makes no difference whatsoever. What counts is that Alvarezos does not like you. By his reasoning, to stretch the word, whoever does not totally and publicly support the regime is totally against it and must be disposed of, one way or another. If it ever came to your word against his, whom do you suppose they would believe? They watched your every move. Your office at the university and your classroom were bugged. They recorded every remark. That's why they know what you discussed with your students, and they interpreted all that to their liking. My ingenious friend, you were such an easy target for them. They could count on your response to whatever circumstance presented to you with reason, selflessness, and objectivity, they could flank you with almost any devious stratagem without the least suspicion on your part."

"My dear Vikas, I do realize that, yet if they wanted so much to write me off, why did they give me the seat of economics to begin with? Why did they give me this position?"

"Who knows, my dear friend, remember where the logic stops the protocol of the army begins. It is strange even to hear these words from a man who made his life serving the army of his country, isn't? But allow me to continue: your intelligent perspective and enthusiasm were contagious and disarming. I was, myself, carried away to the point of forgetting how ruthless the government can be. I mentioned earlier that our conversations at my villa might have been monitored. It seems almost a certainty. It puts me in the position of, even with the best of intentions toward you, having aided them in their miserable plot to trap you and discredit you."

"On the contrary, had I never expressed my ideas to you, you would not be involved as you are now . . ."

"All this about a United Europe, this is just a manipulation to their benefit so they can use it as an excuse to hold you here. Those discussions with your students were nothing improper at all. A government like this has no need of legitimate reason. They do what they wish blatantly and dare anyone to do anything."

"Part of me has known this all along, I suppose."

"That part of you should have been engaged as your bodyguard. And the part of me that listened to your voice of reason should have known better. This is a time in which intelligent thought is not only undesirable but inimical to the regime. It must be silenced, exiled, excised at any cost. The cost has been high already, as you know only too well."

"Yes, however, for myself, I can't regret anything. I have never wished jeopardy for others. I was born the way I am. I have to register exists around me. In part, too, is native intelligence to weigh and evaluate what I register. My studies and my choice to teach were simply a following of my strongest propensities. Here and there I suppose I have occasionally stumbled, but there is a sanctity I hope I have never violated: my intellectual integrity. To most on this earth, that isn't worth a hell of a lot. Most people choose very different priorities and will compromise almost anything to serve their interests. No two men obey exactly the same mandates. I have tried to do as my intelligence commanded. To my distress, and alas, to that of many others, like yourself, who have nothing but my welfare in mind, my duty is counter to the power structure that prevails in this nation. Elsewhere, or even here at another time, my views could be consonant to those at the controls. Let's not forget that, Colonel. Remember what Cavafis says, eh?

> "And greater honor still is due them
> When they foresee (and many do foresee)
> That Ephialtes finally will appear,
> And that the Medes, at last, will get through."

During the remainder of the precious half hour, Vikas explains the details of Petros' theoretical release: No trial. No publicity. In the lowest possible profile, Petros Spathis will be evacuated, as if he had never been confined, as if he had never said anything blasphemous to his students. But, reinstatement of his position at the school will be out of the question. Petros tells Vikas, "If I return to the island to work with my father, I will be under the nose of the mayor; perhaps my very presence will attract undue attention to my innocent family. What are the odds against my slipping out of the country? I'll go back to Vancouver with Samantha, my wife."

"Who is Samantha?"

Petros gives him in a few words regarding Samantha and her plans, and Vikas is really surprised to hear the detail.

"Back to Vancouver sounds like the best bet for you right now. I will check. One thing at a time."

"Thank you with all my heart, Colonel."

"Guard, you may return him to his cell." The guard approaches and Vikas then whispers to Petros, "I'll see you soon and free."

Back in the cell, Petros feels diminished to a cinder by the intensity of the day's metamorphoses of possibility: *321, in a few days I will be legitimately free!* He says "free" aloud. He envisions the word, the shape of the word, in three dimensions, whirling slowly, certainly, gracefully in the green fathoms of an oscilloscope. So many magnificent connotations of that word, yet it escapes them all and revolves, governed by no gravity, a voluptuous form representing itself. *Responsibility shorts the circuit of reverie, 321!*

Petros' mind and dish begin to sculpt a message. In code, is the tap or interval more eloquent?

"321...321!"

"Yes. Not so loud"

"Cannot follow plan."

"What?"

"Will not be with you."

"Fool. What happened?"

"Changes."

"Do they know our plan?"

"No."

"One slip. You are finished. "

"Don't worry. Changes have only to do with me."

"Pity you . . . fool."

"What?"

"Pity you. You would stay here rest of your life for some . . . idea."

"None of your damned business."

"Pity you . . . always be poor and insignificant."

"What?"

"Thinker."

Petros is unaware how long he remains there, with dish in hand and the words rebounding from the shadowy ineffable dark canyons to the surface of consciousness. *You will always be a poor and insignificant thinker.* Blood mushrooms up from all his extremities until the distended veins on his forehead, feeling like hammers against the skull, his mouth opens and the room balloons with the primal howl that only one in extremis can produce and all the languages of the earth together could never describe.

A silence becomes coherent as the previous incoherence engulfs him. Minutes pass and no guard opens the door to see if yet another prisoner has cracked. Petros smiles a little and settles on the bed. *A poor and insignificant thinker,* he thinks. "Inside, here, revolutionary, my Molotov-cocktail neighbor. I'm no poorer, no more insignificant than you. When each of us, by our methods, gets outside this place, we shall see. Perhaps one day we'll meet and compare properties."

Standing tiptoe on his bed, he gazes out from behind the bars of his window into the yard. The Mediterranean sun is flooded, overwhelmed with an almost ominous vitality and warmth. Petros' inner dialogue eclipses the scene, and he enters different place: a world without sun whose dimensions are the same as this cell which he has come to know more intimately than he intended. The planet his imagination stages is one which astronomers would describe as "lifeless," and accelerating into cold, darkness, death; with trees, whose roots have long ago grown too arthritic with decay to hold the ground, lie like jackstraws cast by a Titan. The seas, once so vividly memorial, have been supplanted by lacunae beyond conjure in their depth and breadth. Bloated animals are everywhere, and scent of the ephemeral is heavy upon the strange, almost visible, breeze that seems to stalk Petros despite his changes of direction.

Among the planetary wreckage and offal, a man makes his way toward Petros. As he draws near enough for Petros to make out his jagged features, Petros' fears substantiate: the man is Professor Spathis; a man at the bottom of his well of solitude, in desperate search of others alive in this estate of mind to which he has fallen heir. He finds none but himself. He only has his anathematic thoughts for company.

It would be good to sustain solitude without loneliness, to wrap oneself securely in a robe of singularity, to loose the mind from the short tether prescribed by social order, to shed the body and follow the mind through its labyrinth of abstractions, to follow and follow through the passageways that are, at once, all chaos and all order.

But then there is Samantha and all those who have taken him up as an ideological sword against the corrupt machine. Too often the mortal encumbrances override Petros—it must be possible to revere emptiness, to draw pleasure from it. Continuance of life is out of the question otherwise.

As he sits again on the bed, the idea of ecclesiastical creation slips into his mind, almost a counterweight to the previous tableau. He gazes at the cluster of his thumb and two fingers. "Ah, great, great are your wondrous works, Kyrie."

Two prisoners have escaped. Two days of rampage and panic among the prison personnel pass. Like all other prisoners, Petros is repeatedly questioned. The guards are far more interested in simply appearing to be busy than in the answers Petros confesses to them.

By the third day, their routine is reinstated. Despite the return of silence, Petros sleeps poorly that night.

In the morning, Demetre Vikas brings breakfast of tea, olives, and bread.

"Morning, Demetre. I didn't realize you were on duty today."

The young man nods, pauses then he blurts, "Dead... Father... We buried him yesterday morning. I..." His words freeze.

"What?"

"Day before yesterday... I... all of us were here at the prison on twenty-four-hour call because of the two who escaped. But we didn't find them, you know, we..."

"You are drifting, Demetre, tell me about your father."

"Anagnostis, our villa keeper, found him in our boat. Father loved to work on the boat, even when it needed no repair. Working with his hands was good for him. While he was fiddling around, he could think of other things... He was shot by a long-range rifle. Police say they are investigating. You can be sure there won't be any clues."

"I cannot believe what you just told me."

"I wouldn't lie, Professor. I would no more lie to you than my father would."

"No, no, you misunderstood me. Your father was a man of great heart and great honesty. I'll clarify: for the military dictatorship to execute one of their own senior officers... My God, the bastards are collectively demented. They've unleashed a political form so addicted to blood that when the quarry presents itself to its predacious taste, it begins to eat itself alive."

"I've got to go. I'm certain they're keeping a close watch on me, now that they have... Father..."

"No doubt you are right. Please go."

"If you need anything, tell me when I bring your lunch, I've requested leave for this evening."

The door closes and locks. Petros is suddenly possessed by an almighty itch. He attempts to scratch his entire body at once: he jams his back into the door frame, rakes his chest with his fingernails, tears at the back of one itching hand with the other, digs at one shin with the other foot. His tea dances in the cup; the bed is convulsing. He is part of a grotesque puppet show directed by an impalpable and merciless puppeteer. Bit by bit, his body is slipping away, drifting outside the radiance of his control.

The plague of itching ceases abruptly, leaving him with red streaks and drops of blood on his chest, arms, and face that testify the phenomenon. The compulsions were independent of his mind, as if trapped inside the cab of a huge construction crane with no operator. Petros gazes dazedly through the windshield of his eyes, observes his body as if it is an exotic animal he has encountered for the first time. The distance between his shoulder and fingertips is astoundingly amplified, and even the most trivial movement occurs in terrifying slow motion.

His arm lifts through the air in the room, over the canyon-like distance between his bed and table, to pick up the diary. But then the presence of the food registers in his body, and the first impetus is erased beneath stronger charge of the second. The hand puts the diary aside.

After breakfast, it takes an eternity to light a cigarette. Out of nostalgia for the familiar, the body begins to heed the mind once again.

The pencil comes to hand and he writes: "I have become life's dupe. I have, with great perseverance, endeavored to act as intercessor between questions and their answers. In this liaison, it was revealed to me that there is but one question, and it cannot be expressed in any language. To the question, there is an answer: I am the answer ... One could postulate that I have won. However, I was never informed that the prize for victory is death. On the other hand, death, compliments of the dictatorship, is no more a certainty than my release."

He closes the diary and stands on the headboard to feed on the view of the sun brimming over the courtyard just once more. He wishes to capture the image at its richest within the coasts of memory. Then he curses himself: "What the hell am I doing? Sentencing myself to death a priori?"

His leg muscles stiffen from standing so he begins pacing to loosen them.

But when Colonel Vikas appears inside the locked cell, even the body is astounded and comes to a dead halt. The colonel looks exactly as he did when last Petros saw him: lightning-white hair, blue eyes so deep with sadness and regret yet mixed with warmth and light. This man is a Saint.

"Spathis, remember that you have won." Thereupon the shade dematerializes. If it was a shade. At lunch, Petros asks the young Vikas just to leave the tray. He isn't hungry.

"My pass for tonight has been approved. Is there any way I might be of service to you, Professor?"

"Yes, I would like to ask you a favor, if it isn't an imposition, and if it won't place you even deeper in personal jeopardy. You must not take risks on my account. Is that understood?"

"Very well."

"I need only for this diary to be placed in the hands of a girl."

"Glad to. I can deliver it this evening. Just give me directions."

A few pages from the last the diary speaks directly to Samantha: "My existence has been butchered by duties; every quarter, eighth, sixteenth of me has served so many responsibilities. And now, now it is clear that the only durable part left of me belongs exclusively to you. Circumstances seem to dictate that your faith and patience will only be rewarded by our permanent separation. I love you, if insignificant thinkers are allowed that emotion."

The remainder of the day lurches by. Petros' thoughts are partly carved, then abandoned, and daylight nightmares fail to frighten him. He chain smokes mindlessly.

The essential Petros Spathis is very far from his cell. Petros has molted into this obsolete, ontological exoskeleton.

"*Remember Petros, you have won.*" By all means, my dead, dead Vikas, I have. My life has added yet another Pyrrhic victory to the steep slopes of humanistic slag."

Farther away from cell 322 and the man inside it, the captain warden of the prison has a strange visitor this morning: Colonel Alvarezos in uniformed attire, all his décor on display. The captain stands attention and salutes. The colonel of the A2 intelligence service sits down.

"You have a professor here, I believe," says the colonel.

"Yes, Colonel."

"Considering all the upheaval we had the last few days with the polytechnic school students there are so many bad influences out there, and it is a serious matter. All the enemies of our country have to be eradicated. They are like a disease, like cancer, and they feed on the minds of our people. You know what is expected of you. There is a rumor that he has a wife, a Canadian who is really getting on our nerves. We may have to act quicker than normal because we don't want the Canadian embassy phoning and telling their lies in order to have this miasma freed. I expect you to act today."

The captain stands in attention again and shouts, "Yes, sir, everything will be done. Today."

Farther away from the captain's office, prisoner 322 stands as his door opens and young Vikas serves him his tea and bread with eight olives as always.

"How are you today, Professor?"

"Fine, Demetre, fine. Thank you. News?"

"A letter here from the girl I gave the diary."

"Oh, thank you."

Petros takes the letter.

"I'll be off, then. I'll see you at noon."

Petros reads the letter again and again, as if to memorize its contents for an examination. Then he pockets the letter and begins his habitual pacing, leaving streams and loops of smoke behind him.

Approximately halfway between breakfast and lunch, young Vikas returns, accompanied by the captain warden in full uniform, as if they have returned from an official gathering. Petros is surprised both are wearing their uniforms. Maybe they are on their way to a ceremony, perhaps a formal inspection by some VIP. Vikas carries his rifle and the captain has his handgun in the holster.

"Come along," the captain wears his officiousness like a decoration.

Petros dons his jacket and starts down the corridor ahead of them. "Surely they can't still suppose I know anything about that damned escape. How can they bear hearing themselves ask the same questions over and over?"

They pass through the dim pools of light and the dark interstices between them—it is as if they are phasing through a Hegelian dialectic: pool-darkness-pool-darkness-pool-thesis-darkness-antithesis-darkness-synthesis-darkness . . .

Young Vikas and the captain walk in time, in the custom of the military. Petros finds the regularity of the footsteps and their echoes maddening and tries to establish a cadence at odds with theirs, but in his confusion of footsteps with echoes, finds himself back in step with them again and again.

At the intersection of another corridor, Petros is ordered to stop. He expects to be led to the interrogation room but young Vikas opens a door to a new dim corridor, leading to a zone of the building Petros has never visited before. Soon, a stairwell appears in the echoing gloom, and Petros, having no choice, descends.

The reek of sewer arises around him, enters him, and ingests him. Behind, he hears young Vikas start to gag and then stifle it. He counts fifteen steps before his feet discover a floor once again.

Here, light is even dimmer because of the foul mist above the streaming sewer, glittering its black way past him and on.

He pauses, but the captain pushes him from behind and prods him on.

Young Vikas' voice comes to him through the mist over Petros' shoulder: "I must refuse, Captain."

"You understand this is insubordination," replies his superior.

"Yes, Sir."

"Go back and send for Silva. Wait for me in my office."

As Vikas' footsteps echo and converge to a vanishing point, he hears the captain hissing something to him. "Keep moving, 322, on, on, move on."

Then, a skewer of an incandescent sound.
A blazing implosion of the inside planet.
An island sword shaped, becalmed, bewildered.
The detestable mist . . . lifting and lifting.